P9-CAL-538

THE WRECKING CREW

#2

THE BOOK EXCHANGE #15
in the great Matt Helm
PAPERBACKS SOLD AND TRADED
suspense series
1150 MAIN ST.
COR. GROOM & MAIN
BAKER, LA. 70714

75¢

"The appearance of a new Matt Helm story is always good news." —CHICAGO TRIBUNE

donald hamilton

the
wrecking
crew

A FAWCETT GOLD MEDAL BOOK
Fawcett Publications, Inc., Greenwich, Conn.

Chapter One

I AWOKE EARLY, shaved, dressed, draped myself with cameras and equipment, and went on deck to record our entry into the port of Gothenburg. I couldn't think of a likely market for the shots, but I was supposed to be an eager and ambitious free-lance photographer, and I'd be expected to be alert to the chance that somebody would fall overboard or the ship would hit something.

Nothing happened, and after we were safely docked I went down to breakfast, after which I came back up to the smoking room for passport inspection. Finally I was shunted down the gangplank into the arms of the Swedish customs, where I braced myself to justify my possession of a thousand bucks' worth of photographic gear and several hundred rolls of film, having been warned that European countries are touchy about this sort of thing. It was a bum steer. Nobody paid any attention to the cameras and film. The only part of my belongings that caused a mild official interest was the guns.

I explained that an editor in New York had arranged with a sporting character in Stockholm to have an import permit waiting for me at the dock. I was thereupon escorted down the long shed to an office where a blond young fellow shortly produced a document authorizing Herr Matthew L. Helm, of Santa Fe, New Mexico, USA, to transport into the kingdom of Sweden one *räffla gevär, Winchester, kaliber .30–06,* and one *hagelbössa, Remington, kaliber 12.*

The youthful customs man checked the serial numbers of the rifle and shotgun, then laid the weapons on a platform scale, wrote down the total weight in kilograms, consulted a table with this figure, and announced that the duty would be thirteen crowns. Having already learned that the Swedish crown was worth approximately twenty cents, I couldn't feel that the tariff was exorbitant, but it did seem like a funny way to assess it.

As I left the office, I soothed my conscience with the thought that by not declaring the aluminum-framed, five-shot Smith and Wesson .38 Special concealed in my luggage, I wasn't really cheating the Swedish government of much money—less than two bits, in fact—since it was a very light little gun.

It had been Mac's idea. "Your bona-fide literary and photographic background is going to come in very handy on this job," he'd said, giving me my instructions in his Washington office. "To be perfectly frank, it's the chief reason you were selected, in spite of the length of time that's passed since you were associated with us last. There's also the fact that you already know the language, after a fashion, and we haven't many operatives who do."

He'd looked up at me across the desk—a spare, gray-haired man of indeterminate age, with coal-black eyebrows and cold black eyes. Somehow he always managed to arrange his offices, wherever they might be (I could remember one in London with a grim view of bombed-out buildings) so that he had a window behind him, making it hard to read his expression against the light, which I suppose was the idea. "You've done articles for outdoor magazines in the past," he'd said. "What's more logical than for you to be working on a couple of hunting pieces in addition to your main photographic assignment? I'll get in touch with some people and fix it up for you."

I said, "There's going to be a lot of red tape with the guns. Other countries are more sensitive about firearms than we are."

"Precisely," he said. "That's just the point. You take a lot of trouble to get the proper papers for your hunting arms, all open and innocent, and who's going to suspect you of packing a revolver and a knife as well? Anyway, they've got some pretty wild terrain up there in northern Sweden where you're going. Who knows, a high-powered rifle may be just what you'll need."

It had still seemed like an unnecessary complication to me. I hadn't looked forward to juggling a rifle and a shotgun, plus a lot of hunting paraphernalia, in addition to the camera junk I was already saddled with by my role as photographer. However, as Mac had pointed out, I'd been out of touch for a long time; I wasn't familiar with the subtleties of peacetime operation. But I did remember

6

clearly from the war that there were limits to the amount of argument Mac would tolerate from a subordinate, particularly when he felt he was being extremely clever.

"Okay," I said hastily. "You're the boss, sir."

I hadn't wanted him to change his mind about putting me back to work. And now I was landing on European soil again, after better than fifteen years, with the same old feeling that everybody was looking at me and my belongings with knowing, X-ray eyes.

There was bright sunshine outside the customs shed—well, as bright as you get in the fall that far north. It would probably have seemed like a pale and wintry day, back home in New Mexico. There was a wide, cobblestoned street outside, full of weird, left-handed traffic. The Swedes, along with the British, persist in driving on the opposite side of the street from practically everybody else in the world.

There were two-and four-wheeled vehicles in just about equal numbers, with some oddly shaped three-wheelers thrown in for good measure. The taxi that took me to the railroad station was a German Mercedes. The train itself had an old-fashioned, unstreamlined look that was kind of refreshing. I disposed of my heavier baggage with the proper official, and started to get into one of the cars, but stepped back to let a woman board first.

She was quite a handsome young woman—from where I stand, thirty still qualifies as young—and she was wearing a severely tailored blue suit that did justice to her figure in a nice, understated way; but her hair, under the little blue tweed hat that matched her suit, was also blue, which seemed odd to me. Of course there was really no reason why a good-looking female of youthful appearance whose hair had turned white prematurely shouldn't dye the stuff blue if she wanted to.

I followed her aboard. She apparently knew her way around Swedish rolling stock better than I did. I lost track of her in the unfamiliar surroundings. It had been a long time since I'd last patronized a European railroad. This car was divided into small eight-passenger compartments marked either *Rökare* or *Icke Rökare*. Remembering from my Minnesota boyhood that *röka* means smoke in Swedish, and *icke* means no, I had no trouble understanding the distinction, particularly since other signs gave the translation in German, French, and English.

I selected an empty nonsmoker and settled down by the window, which could be raised and lowered by means of a leather strap about four inches wide. I couldn't recall the last time I'd been on a train that wasn't sealed up tight for air conditioning, but of course they wouldn't need that here, in the shadow of the Arctic Circle. It was a long ride to Stockholm, through green, partly forested country interrupted by a multitude of lakes and streams, and accented with red barns and orange-red tile roofs.

Around three in the afternoon, a little late, having traversed the entire width of the country from west to east, the train entered the capital of Sweden across a long bridge over water; but it was twenty minutes more before I could extract my junk from the baggage room and transfer it to a waiting taxi. I'd got over my first feeling of stage fright. Nobody seemed to be paying the slightest attention to me now, except for some kids intrigued by my big Western hat. One of them came over and bobbed his blond head politely.

"Yes," I said, "what is it?"

"Är farbror en cowboy?" he asked.

In addition to having had some contact with the language as a boy, I'd been given a quick refresher course—not only in the language, but in other subjects as well—before being sent out. But of course I wasn't supposed to understand a word, and somebody might be watching, so I looked blank.

"Sorry, I don't read you," I said. "Can't you put it into English?"

A woman's voice said, behind me, "He wants to know if you're a cowboy."

I looked around, and there she was again, blue suit, blue hair, and all. Bumping into her a second time didn't please me a bit. It wasn't a contact, because there was nobody here I was scheduled to meet in this manner; and I'd once survived a war mainly by putting no faith whatever in the power of coincidence. It still seemed like a sound principle to follow.

"Thank you, ma'am," I said. "Please tell the kid that I'm sorry, but I never roped a steer in my life. The hat and the boots are just for show."

This was another of Mac's fancy ideas. I was supposed to be something of a rustic Gary Cooper character, as well as a hunter and a camera-clicking screwball. Well, I had

8

the height for it, if no other qualifications; but I couldn't help feeling, with this woman's eyes upon me, that the act I was being asked to put on was unnecessarily detailed and complicated, not to mention corny. However, I'd asked for the job—after first turning it down twice—so I wasn't in a position to complain.

The woman laughed, and turned to speak to the boy, in swift and fluent Swedish that had, however, a trace of an American accent. He looked disappointed, and ran off to tell his pals that I was a phony. The woman turned back to me, smiling.

"You broke his heart," she said.

"Yes," I said. "Well, thanks a lot for interpreting."

I got into the cab, leaving her standing there. She had quite a pretty smile, but if she had some reason besides my masculine appeal for wanting to talk to me, she'd undoubtedly turn up again; and if she didn't, I had no time for her. I mean, I've never had any sympathy for agents who can't refrain from complicating their jobs with irrelevant females. The relevant ones usually present problems enough.

I rode away without looking back, bracing myself against the psychological impact of the cockeyed traffic, which seemed even more unnatural because the cab was an ordinary American Plymouth with the steering wheel in the usual place. If they had to drive contrary to everyone else, you'd think they'd at least shift the driver over to where he could see the road. In addition to cars, the streets swarmed with ordinary bicycles, bikes with little motors, motor scooters, and full-grown motorcycles driven at furious speed by kids in round white crash helmets and black leather jackets.

At the hotel, I had to register on a police card that required me to state, among other things, where I'd come from last, how long I was staying here, and where I planned to go next. I was a little shocked to meet this sort of police-state red tape here, in time of peace. The Swedes were, after all, supposed to be among the most secure and democratic people in Europe, if not in the world, but apparently a foreigner had to be reported to the cops every time he changed hotels; and I wasn't forgetting that bringing an ordinary rifle and shotgun into the country had demanded the equivalent of an act of Congress. I couldn't help won-

9

dering what they were afraid of. Probably people like me.

My room turned out to be big and pleasant, overlooking one of the wide, picturesque estuaries that seemed to be just about everywhere you went in Stockholm—my taxi ride had confirmed my first impression that the city was half water and bridges. I got rid of the bellboy and looked at my watch. Eventually I'd have to report my arrival, as a matter of interdepartmental courtesy, to certain fellow-citizens on the spot, but this was a little detail I could postpone without a qualm of conscience. The less I had to do with professional diplomats and intelligence people, the better I liked it.

However, I also had an appointment of sorts directly connected with the job, and the train had made me later than I'd expected. I picked up the phone.

"I'd like to speak with Mrs. Taylor," I said. "I believe she's staying here. Mrs. Louise Taylor?"

"Mrs. Taylor?" The desk clerk's voice, speaking English, had a strong British accent with Swedish overtones. It made an odd combination. "Righto," he said. "Room 311. I'll connect you, sir."

Standing there, waiting for the call to be put through, I became aware that someone had stepped out of the closet behind me.

Chapter Two

A CANNY secret-agent type would, of course, have looked the place over carefully before turning his back on the closet and bathroom doors. Under other circumstances, I might even have done so myself, but I was playing a part, and my script didn't call for any displays of professional vigilance. Mac had been emphatic on this point.

"You've now been given a thorough refresher course of training, courtesy of Uncle Sam," he said at my final briefing. "It's possible that Uncle, being a peaceful sort, wouldn't approve of everything in the curriculum, but what Uncle doesn't know won't hurt him. Security has its advantages, and we're very top-secret here. We're supposed to be developing some kind of a mystery weapon, I believe. Well, one might call it that. After all, the greatest mystery on earth, and the most dangerous weapon, is man himself."

Having delivered himself of this weighty philosophy, he looked at me expectantly across the desk. I said, "Yes, sir."

Mac grimaced. "I have your record here. It's quite outstanding. I haven't seen a worse one in a long time. Your reflexes and reaction times are lousy. Your score with a pistol, on all courses of fire, is pitiful. With a rifle you're a little better, but then, practically anybody can shoot a rifle. With a knife, thanks to your long arms, you almost reached adequacy, it says here, once you stopped falling over your big feet. At unarmed combat, thanks again to your ridiculous height and reach, you finally succeeded in scaling the highest peaks of mediocrity. Your physical condition was deplorable when we got you, and it's still nothing to cheer about. You've lost fifteen pounds, and could dispense with another ten without missing an ounce. What the devil have you been doing with yourself all these years, just sitting around on your rear elevation?"

"That's about it, sir," I said.

I'd been about to protest that my record couldn't possibly be as bad as he claimed. As a matter of fact, for a man coming back to the organization after a fifteen-year layoff, I thought I'd done fairly well. About to say as much, I'd changed my mind, realizing that he wasn't asking me, he was telling me. Regardless of what scores I'd actually made, this was what was going into the files, just in case somebody came snooping. He was being clever again. For some reason he considered it advantageous for me to seem practically helpless.

"The recommendation of the staff was unanimous," Mac went on, poker-faced. "Not one of them would take the responsibility of clearing you for a dangerous mission." He shoved the papers away from him. "They're a bunch of fools," he said. "I told them my reasons for wanting you, and still they send me this! We've got so much red tape, it's a wonder we get anything done. Nowadays everybody's supposed to have a signed certificate from a doctor, a psychologist, and six coaches and trainers, before he's permitted to cross the street to fetch the evening paper. Remember the time I sent you across the Channel with a man we called Vance? You had a half-healed bullet hole in your chest, and he had his arm in a sling. It made your impersonations of German soldiers on convalescent leave much more convincing, and there's no evidence that it affected your performances adversely. I don't put much stock in physical condition. A man's mental condition is what counts."

"Yes, sir," I said. He was getting wordy in his old age. He'd never talked this much during the war.

He frowned at me for a moment. "Vance is still with us, incidentally," he said. "If you've forgotten what he looks like—we've all changed a bit since those days—you can identify him by the scar just above the elbow where the bone came out through the skin. Keep that in mind. He'll be your direct contact with me, if for any reason you should find it inadvisable to use the regular channels of communication you've been told about." He pursed his lips. "Of course, other departments have much greater facilities for transmitting messages than we have, and they give us wonderful cooperation, but you might just feel like sending something meant for my eyes alone. Or I might want to send something for yours. Vance will pass it on, either way. He's operating on the continent, but the plane service is excellent, if you should need assistance."

"Yes, sir," I said.

He glanced at the training-course records again. "As for this stuff," he said, "whether or not it's precisely accurate doesn't matter, since the first thing I want you to do, when you leave this room, is forget everything you've just been taught. If I'd thought this job required a man trained to razor-edge perfection, I wouldn't have picked one well along in his thirties, a man who's been outside the organization, wielding nothing more lethal than camera and typewriter, for fifteen years. Do you understand what I'm trying to tell you?"

"Not completely, sir," I said. "You'll have to spell it out for me."

He said, "I had you put through the mill for your own sake. I couldn't in good conscience send you out so rusty and out of condition you'd get yourself killed. Besides, we've developed some new techniques since your time, which I thought you'd like to know about. But in many ways you'd have been better prepared for the job at hand if you'd spent the past month in a hotel room with a bottle and a blonde. Now you'll have to use restraint. Don't betray yourself by showing off any of the pretty tricks you've just learned. If somebody wants to follow you, let them follow; you don't even know they're there. What's more, you don't care. If they want to search your belongings, don't set any traps for them. If you should get involved in a fight—God forbid—forget about weapons except in a clear and desperate emergency. And don't give any unnecessary judo demonstrations, either. Just lead with your right and take your licking like a man. Do I make myself clear?"

"Well, I begin to see daylight through the mists, sir."

He said, "I was sorry to hear that your wife has left you, but this project ought to take your mind off your marital troubles for a while." He glanced at me sharply. "I suppose that's why you suddenly changed your mind about coming back to work, after turning me down twice."

"Yes, sir," I said.

He frowned at me. "It's been a long time, hasn't it? I don't mind saying that I'm glad to have you. You may be a trifle soft in the body, but you can't possibly be as bad as the youngsters we get nowadays, who are practically all

13

soft in the head. . . . You'll be taking considerable risk, of course," he went on more briskly. "I feel that the risk will be lessened by a deliberate show of ineptness, but this means that you'll be a sitting duck for anybody who really wants you out of the way. You'll have to give the other fellow all the breaks. But it's a foregone conclusion that they're going to test you out carefully before they accept you as harmless, and you don't want to scare them off. We've got a good cover for you, but one clever, professional move on your part will blow it instantly. You don't know anything like that, except what you've seen in the movies. You're just a hick free-lance photographer on his first assignment for a big New York magazine, aching to make good. That's all you are. Don't forget it for a minute. The job, and maybe even your life, may depend on it."

"Yes, sir."

"Your target," Mac said, "is a man named Caselius. At least that's the only name he uses that seems to be known. He undoubtedly has others. He's apparently a pretty good man in his line, which is espionage. He's bothering our earnest counter-intelligence people no end, so that they've finally overcome their humanitarian scruples and put in a request for us to take action. The fact that the man seems to be dangerous may have influenced them slightly. They've lost a number of agents who got too close to this mysterious fellow; and there was an incident last year involving a magazine writer, a chap named Harold Taylor, who published a popular article on Soviet espionage in general and Mister Caselius in particular. It was the first time, to our knowledge, that the name had appeared in print.

"Shortly thereafter Taylor and his wife were accidentally sprinkled with a full clip of submachine-gun bullets while stopped at a road block in the wrong part of Germany. A careless sentry and a mechanical malfunction was the official explanation. There seems to be little doubt among our people that Caselius was responsible. Apparently Taylor had learned too much, somehow. This is the angle you're supposed to exploit."

"Exploit how?" I asked. "It's been a long time since I've used a ouija board, sir."

Mac ignored my feeble attempt at witticism. "Taylor was killed instantly, according to the reports. His wife, however, was only wounded, and survived. She was returned to our side of the so-called curtain after considerable delay, for which medical reasons were given. There were many official apologies and expressions of regret, of course. She is now in Stockholm, Sweden, ostensibly trying to continue her late husband's writing career on her own hook. She has turned out a magazine article on iron mining in northern Sweden that requires photographic illustrations. I have arranged for you to be the man assigned by the magazine in question to take the pictures.

"Our intelligence people over there seem to think there's something fishy about the accident to her husband, about her long detention in the East German hospital, and even about her sudden decision to take up article writing. In any case, you are to use her as a starting point. Guilty or innocent, she may lead you, somehow, to Caselius. Or you may have to figure out another angle. How you do it is your business. When you've made your touch, report back to me."

The word seemed to bring a slight chill into the office. The Russians prefer the word liquidate. The syndicate boys call it making a hit. But we'd always referred to it as a touch, for no reason anybody'd ever figured out.

"Yes, sir," I said.

"Eric," he said, using my code name, as was our practice.

"Sir?"

"A little of that sirring goes a long way, Eric. We're not in the army now."

"No, sir," I said. It was an old running joke between us, dating back to the time I'd first come to the outfit as an overeager young second lieutenant, happy to be singled out for special duty, even though I didn't know what it was or why I'd been chosen. "I'll certainly remember that, sir," I said with a straight face.

He gave me a glimpse of his rare, wintry smile. "Just a few more things before you go," he said. "You haven't had many dealings with these people. Just remember that they're as tough as the Nazis ever were and maybe even a shade smarter; at least they don't go around claiming to be supermen. Remember that you aren't quite as young as you were when we used to send you over into occupied France. And, finally, remember that you could get by with certain things in wartime that won't pass in time of peace. This is a friendly country you'll be visiting. You not only have to find your man and make the touch, you have to make it

15

look good. You can't shoot it out with their police and run for the border, if you make a mistake." He hesitated. "Eric."

"Sir?"

"About your wife. Would it help if I were to speak with her?"

"I doubt it," I said. "All you could do would be to tell her the truth about the kind of work we did during the war, and that's just what she's recently discovered for herself. She can't make herself forget it. It got so she couldn't stand to have me come near her." I shrugged my shoulders. "Well, it was bound to happen. I just tried to kid myself I could get away from it for good. I really had no business getting married and having a family. But thanks for the offer."

He said, "If you get into trouble, we'll do what we can unofficially, but officially we never heard of you. Good luck."

All of this, some of it quite beside the point, went through my mind as I stood there holding the phone. The person behind me had made no real sound, but I knew quite well that I had company. I didn't turn, but casually stretched out a foot, hooked a chair within reach, and sat down, as a woman's voice came over the wire.

"Yes?"

"Mrs. Taylor?" I said.

"Yes, this is Mrs. Taylor."

Well, it wasn't the woman with the blue hair. This was a much deeper voice than the one I'd heard at the railroad station. I got an impression of a brusque and businesslike female who didn't approve of wasting time with idle amenities. Perhaps I was prejudiced by my knowledge that Louise Taylor had been a journalist's wife and had done some writing herself. On the whole, my experience with literary ladies hasn't been encouraging.

"This is Matt Helm, Mrs. Taylor," I said.

"Oh, yes, the photographer," she said. "I've been expecting you. Where are you now?"

"Right in the hotel," I said. "The train was late; I just got in. If you have some time to spare, Mrs. Taylor, I'd like to discuss the article with you before I fly north to do the pix."

She hesitated, as if I'd said something surprising. Then

16

she said, "Why don't you come to my room, and we'll talk about it over a drink? But I must warn you, Mr. Helm, if you're a bourbon man, you'll have to bring your own. I'm hoarding my last bottle. They never heard of the stuff over here. I've got plenty of Scotch, though."

"Scotch will do me fine, Mrs. Taylor," I said. "I'll be down as soon as I put on a clean shirt."

I hung up. Then I turned from the instrument casually. It wasn't the easiest thing in the world to do, and I was careful to move slowly enough, I hoped, not to startle my unknown roommate into precipitate action.

I could have saved myself the trouble. She was just standing there, empty-handed and harmless—if any pretty woman can be called harmless—with her expensive tweed suit and severe silk blouse and soft blue hair. Well, I'd told myself that if she really had some reason for wanting to talk with me, she'd turn up again.

Chapter Three

WE FACED each other for a moment in silence, while I dropped my jaw and widened my eyes to register the emotions proper to finding myself—surprise, surprise— not alone. It gave me a chance to look her over more carefully than I had hitherto done.

The hair was really blue, I saw; it had not been an optical illusion, and it was not merely that vague rinse that gray-haired women often apply for reasons incomprehensible to the male of the species. This was, as I'd judged, prematurely white hair, very fine in texture, meticulously waved and set, and dyed a pale but definite shade of blue. When you got over the initial shock, it looked smart and striking as a frame for her young-looking face and violet-blue eyes. But I can't say I really liked it.

It was an interesting effect, but I'm not partial to women who go in for interesting, artificial, calculated effects. They arouse in me the perverted desire to dump them into the nearest swimming pool, or get them sloppy drunk, or rape them—anything to learn if there's a real woman under all the camouflage.

Having registered surprise, I let myself grin slowly. "Well, well!" I said. "This is real nice, ma'am! I think I'm going to like Stockholm. Is there one of you for every room, or are you just a special treat for visiting Americans?" Then I hardened my voice. "All right, sister, what's the racket? You've been trailing me around ever since I set foot on shore, trying for a pickup. Now you listen carefully. It would be a bad mistake for you to rip that handsome blouse and threaten to start screaming, or have your husband charge in, or whatever similar stunt you have in mind.

"You see, ma'am, all us Americans aren't millionaires, by a long shot. I don't have enough money to make it worth your while, and if I did have I damn well wouldn't pay off anyway. So why don't you just run along and find yourself another sucker?"

She flushed; then she smiled faintly. "You did that very well, Mr. Helm," she said, rather condescendingly. "Just the slightest tension in the shoulders when you realized I was standing here, almost imperceptible. The rest was very convincing. But then, they'd be bound to send a pretty good man after so many had failed, wouldn't they?"

I said, "Ma'am, you've sure got your signals crossed somewhere. I don't know what you're talking about."

She said, "You can drop that phony drawl. I don't think they really talk that way in Santa Fe, New Mexico. You're Matthew Helm, age thirty-six, hair blond, eyes blue, height six-four, weight just under two hundred pounds. That's what it says in the official description we received. But I don't know where you hang two hundred pounds on that beanpole frame, my friend."

She studied me for a moment. "As a matter of fact, you're not really a very good man, are you? According to our information, you're a retread, hauled out of retirement for this job because of your ideal qualifications with respect to background and languages. A trained agent with a genuine record of photo-journalism and a working knowledge of Swedish isn't easy to come by. I suppose they had to do the best they could. Your department warned us that you might need a little nursemaiding, which is why I made a special trip to Gothenburg to keep an eye on you." She frowned. "Just what is your department, anyway? The instructions we received were kind of vague on that point. I thought I knew most of the organizations we might have to work with."

I didn't answer her question. I was reflecting bitterly that Mac seemed to have done a fine job of giving me the reputation of a superannuated stumblebum. Perhaps it was necessary, but it certainly put me on the defensive here. The identity of my visitor was becoming fairly obvious, but it could still be a trick, and I said impatiently:

"Now, look, sister, be nice. Be smart. Go bother the guy in the next room for a while; maybe he likes mysterious female screwballs. I've got a date. You probably heard me make it. Will you get the hell out of here so I can wash up a little, or do I have to call the desk and have them send for a couple of husky characters in white jackets?"

She said, "The word is Aurora. Aurora Borealis. Your orders were to report to me the minute you reached Stockholm. Give me the countersign, please."

That placed her. She was the Stockholm agent I was supposed to notify of my arrival. I said, "The Northern Lights burn brightly in the Land of the Midnight Sun." I must have memorized half a thousand passwords and countersigns in my time, but I still feel like a damn fool when it comes time to give them. This specimen should tell you why—and at that, it isn't half as silly as some I've had to deliver with a straight face.

"Very well," said the woman before me, crisply. She gestured toward the telephone I had recently put down. "Now explain, if you please, why you chose to approach the subject before contacting me as instructed."

She was pushing her authority very hard, and she didn't really have much to push, but Mac had been explicit about what my attitude should be. "You'll just have to grin and bear it," he'd said. "Remember this is peace, God bless it. Be polite, be humble. That's an order. Don't get our dear, dedicated intelligence people all upset or they might wet their cute little lace panties."

Mac didn't ordinarily go in for scatological humor; it was a sign that he felt strongly about the kind of people we had to work with these days. He grimaced. "We've been asked to lend a hand, Eric, but if there's a strong protest locally, we could also be asked to withdraw. There's even a possibility, if you make yourself too unpopular, that some tender soul might get all wrought up and pull strings to embarrass us here in Washington. Every agent must be a public relations man these days." He gave me his thin smile. "Do the best you can, and if you should haul off and clip one of them, please, please be careful not to kill him."

So I held my temper in check, and refrained from pointing out that I was, technically, quite independent of her authority or anybody else's except Mac's. I didn't even bother to tell her that her nursemaiding of me from Gothenburg to Stockholm—as she'd called it—and her presence in my room now, had probably left me with just about as much of my carefully constructed cover as a shelled Texas pecan. She wasn't exactly inconspicuous, with that hair. Nobody watching me could have missed her. Her opposite number on the other team, here in Stockholm, would be bound to know who she was. Any hint of communication between us would make everybody I was to deal with very suspicious indeed.

I was supposed to have got in touch with her by telephone, when I judged it safe. By barging in like this, she'd knocked hell out of most of my plans. Well, it was done, and there was nothing to be gained by squawking about it. I'd just have to refigure my calculations to allow for it, if possible.

I said humbly, "I'm very sorry, Aurora—or should I say Miss Borealis. I didn't mean to —"

She said, "My name is Sara. Sara Lundgren."

"A Svenska girl, eh?"

She said stiffly, "My parents were of Swedish extraction, yes. Just like yours, according to the records. I happen to have been born in New York City, if it's any business of yours."

"None at all," I said. "And I'm truly sorry if I've fouled things up in any way by calling the Taylor woman, but I'd sent her a radiogram from the boat saying I'd be here by three, and the train was late, so I thought I'd better get in touch with her before she got tired of waiting and left the hotel. I'd have checked with you tonight, Miss Lundgren, you may be sure."

"Oh," she said, slightly mollified. "Well, we might have had some important last-minute instructions for you; and I do think orders are made to be obeyed, don't you? In any case I should think you'd want to hear what I know about the situation before you go barging into it like a bull buffalo. After all, this isn't a ladies' tea, you know. The man we're after has already cost us three good agents dead, and one crippled and permanently insane from torture he wasn't supposed to survive—not to mention the Taylor woman's husband. We don't really know what happened to him, except from her story, which may be the truth but probably isn't. I know you were well-briefed before you left the States, but I should think you'd want the viewpoint of the agent on the spot as well."

"Naturally," I said. "I was hoping you could give me a lot of details that weren't in the official reports, Miss Lundgren."

She smiled abruptly. "I suppose I should apologize. I didn't really mean to throw my weight around, but I do

21

like things to be done according to the rules . . . and you did hurt my feelings, you know."

"Hurt your feelings?" I said, surprised. "How? When?"

She laughed. "When a strange lady addresses you in a public place, Mr. Helm, like a railroad station, and smiles her prettiest, you're not supposed to turn on your heel and walk away. It makes her feel . . . well, unattractive. I *was* trying to pick you up; I thought that would be the most convincing way of making contact. Instead, you left me standing there with my mouth open, looking like a fool." She laughed again. "Well, the subject is waiting for you; we'll have to talk later. I run a little dress shop on Johannesgatan—*gata* means street, you know. I live in the apartment above the shop. The stairs are at the side. . . . No, that won't do, will it? You'd better not come there."

After the way she'd already compromised my act, it didn't make much difference. But I said, "It doesn't seem advisable. Although it would be pleasant."

Her smile died. "You can stop *that* right now, my friend. I've been in this work quite a while; and when I make a midnight appointment for business, I assure you that's all it is—business. Anyway, I'm engaged to be married as soon as I've put in my time here. Please understand clearly that just because I don't like a man to walk away from me as you did doesn't mean I want to go to bed with him!"

I said, "It's understood. Sorry."

She said curtly, "You'll probably have dinner with the woman if you can manage, won't you? You'll have lots of technical matters to discuss with her, but please try to keep the conversation out of the boudoir. You seem to fancy yourself as a fast worker, and that may be the way to handle it, all right. But you'll have plenty of time later, if things work out, and I don't want to have to wait all night for you.

"As soon as you can get rid of her, after dinner, go out for a walk. It won't surprise anybody. Everybody walks in this country. You never saw such a bunch of energetic people. When you come out of the hotel, cross the street to the seawall and turn left. Follow the water. There's a kind of park along the shore. After fifty yards of that, there's a phone booth. You've seen their phone booths? On stilts, kind of, with a luminous white globe on top and illuminated advertising on all four sides, under glass. Very gaudy, particularly at night. You can't miss it."

"I'll try not to."

"When you get there, pretend to make a call, and wait," she said. "I'll be somewhere around. I'll contact you as soon as I'm sure you're not being followed." She smiled at me. "I'm sorry if I was unpleasant. I think we're going to get along."

As I watched her leave the room, walking with a restrained and decorous motion of the narrow hips under the tweed skirt, I wasn't a bit sure of that. I've never managed to get along well with any woman who had that kind of a prissy behind.

Chapter Four

WHEN I knocked on the door of Room 311, it was opened for me by a lean dark girl in tight black pants. She was also wearing a loose bulky black sweater and a long cigarette holder. Despite the beatnik get-up, or maybe because of it, she looked much too young to be the woman I'd spoken with on the phone, and I said:

"I'm Matthew Helm. Is Mrs. Taylor here?"

"I'm Lou Taylor," she said, and there was that deep, hoarse voice again. She held out her hand. "Glad to meet you, Helm." I'm always a bit taken aback when a woman shoves her mitt at me like a man, and I guess my face showed it, because the girl laughed huskily and said, "You'll be doing it, too, after you've been here a week. These damn Swedes shake hands at the drop of a hat, males and females both. . . . Well, don't just stand there, come on in. What kind of a crossing did you have?"

"Smooth," I said. "A bit foggy in spots."

"You can count yourself lucky," she said. "The Atlantic can get pretty sloppy at this time of year."

She had closed the door. I followed her deeper into the room. It wasn't laid out quite like mine, but there was a family resemblance. A man was perched on the arm of the only comfortable chair in the place, a big, overstuffed piece by the window. He rose and came forward.

He was tall and big-shouldered and some years my junior, with a handsome boyish face and tightly curling chestnut hair cut quite close to his head as if he was ashamed of it. He was wearing narrow Ivy League gray flannels—coat and pants—a white shirt with a button-down collar, and a bow tie. The tie had been tied by him, not by a machine. I was told by my dad once that a man who tied his own ties was much more likely to be a gentleman than one who did not. Just what constitutes a gentleman in this day and age, the old man didn't bother to say. To him, the distinction was clear. It must have been nice.

The man facing me, gentleman or not, was the kind of guy who makes you wonder instinctively if you can take him barehanded or if you'll need a club. I don't mean that he looked particularly objectionable. He merely oozed that aggressive masculinity that makes such thoughts come into other men's minds. The funny thing was, I'd met him somewhere before. Even if I hadn't vaguely remembered his features, I'd have known by the look of surprised recognition that showed for an instant in his yellowish eyes.

"Mr. Helm," the girl with the cigarette holder said, "I want you to meet Mr. Wellington. Jim, Matt Helm."

We shook hands. His grip was surprisingly gentle, the grip of a man who knows his own strength and guards it carefully. It was a point in his favor, to weigh against his virile good looks.

"Lou tells me you're a photographer," he said.

"That's right," I said.

"Used to take pictures myself for a hobby," he said. "Won half a dozen prizes at our camera club back home in Baltimore, but I guess that's small stuff to you pros. . . . Well, I'll leave you to your business. See you, Lou."

He released my hand and wheeled toward the door, and in that moment I placed him. It had been during the war, at night. They'd brought this big kid up to me on the airfield saying that since I was lone-wolfing it this trip there was plenty of room, and if I didn't mind, it would save their making an extra run. He wasn't one of ours—he was OSS or something—and I wasn't crazy about having any outsiders knowing where I'd been dropped, but there wasn't much I could do about it.

Nobody bothered to introduce us. We didn't have names around that place, anyway; we were just cargo to be delivered. I shook hands with the boy, that was all. He'd been a knuckle grinder back in those days; apparently he'd learned better manners since. Then they called that the plane was ready and he wheeled toward it with that same aggressive football readiness of a big man who expects to be hit hard and intends to stay on his feet nevertheless. . . .

I remembered the rest of that night clearly. We hadn't talked on the way across the Channel. We'd been just two young guys with different destinations, sharing a taxi for a few blocks, and I'd been wondering, as always, if this was the night my chute wouldn't open or I'd land in some hot wires and fry to death. He'd had his own thoughts, of a similar nature, probably. He didn't even wish me good luck when it was time for me to drop, but I didn't hold that against him. We had no sentimental traditions or customs in our organization, but in some outfits, I knew, just as among some hunters, it was considered bad form to wish anybody luck at parting.

"So long, fella," was all he said.

I never have liked people who call me fella, so I just gave him a nod as I went out. The hell with him. If you want to make buddies, join the infantry. The umbrella opened fine, and I landed in an open field, and I never saw the guy again until now.

He turned briefly at the door, waggled his hand in a half salute and looked at me casually, and I knew that he was double-checking, studying me from this new angle to make quite sure. After all, some time had passed. A horse born that night would be a pretty old nag by now. It was a wife and three kids ago for me. But he had a good eye, a trained eye, and he knew me, all right, and he went out without saying a word, which was the significant thing. He had recognized me, but he kept his mouth shut. It could mean a lot of things. After all, I wasn't joyously recalling auld lang syne, either.

"Who's he?" I asked, when he was gone.

"Jim?" Lou Taylor shrugged her shoulders. "Just a friend. He's kind of nice, actually. He's the Stockholm representative for a U.S. plastics firm, if it makes a difference. . . . Scotch or gin? I recommend the Scotch. The gin you get here isn't fit to drink."

"In that case, Scotch," I said.

"I just want to get one thing straight, Helm," she said, turning to face me with the glass in her hand. "On the phone, you sounded as if you were planning to go up to Kiruna all alone. Well, don't kid yourself. This is my article, and I'm going to be right beside you when you shoot the pictures. I don't know much about photography, but I know the stuff I want, and I'm at least going to see that you get it down on film, whether or not it gets used later."

26

Chapter Five

IT CAME so easily and naturally that it caught me by surprise. I'd expected to have to work for it. I'd thought she'd at least try to be cute about it. It was such a simple and obvious test.

"Try her," Mac had said. "If she's willing to let you go up to the Arctic and shoot these mining pictures all by yourself, her article is probably as innocent as it seems, and you're wasting your time. In that case, you'll have to dig up another lead somewhere. But if she insists on coming with you, you may be in business." He hesitated. "Eric."

"Sir?"

"Strictly speaking, the sex of your quarry has not yet been determined. I speak of him as a man only because Taylor's article refers to him as a man. But Taylor's information should not be accepted uncritically. We don't know where he got it or how reliable it is. He may even have had reasons for being deliberately misleading. As for the wife, nobody seems to know too much about her. Apparently she's just an American kid he met in Rome a few years back; everybody was rather surprised when they got married, since he hadn't been considered good matrimonial material." Mac smiled thinly. "Anyway, just because a suspect is female doesn't mean that she can be safely disregarded. Keep it in mind."

I was keeping it in mind as I faced Mrs. Taylor in her hotel room. It wasn't hard to do. She had no appeal for me at the moment. I've never had much use for women in pants. When I mentioned this idiosyncrasy to a psychiatrist friend, he said it was a subconscious defense mechanism against my incipient homosexual tendencies. He had me worried for a while, until I discovered that he explained all human behavior on the grounds of incipient homosexual tendencies. He was even writing a book about his theory, but I don't think he ever finished it. Somebody else beat him to it. The competition in the field of psychiatric theories is fierce these days.

Anyway, a woman in pants has very little interest for me, as a woman, and that goes double for all the strange britches women have taken to parading around in lately. Mrs. Taylor's snugly fitting nether garments—I wouldn't know precisely what to call them—came to an arbitrary end just below her calves, so that they looked like slacks badly shrunk in the wash. She was wearing soft black slippers. Her hair was dark, cut off short, and brushed back over her ears boyishly.

I couldn't help remembering that this was, or had been, a married woman, and wondering what her husband had thought of this get-up. It must have been kind of like going to bed with your kid brother.

I said, "Don't bite me, Mrs. Taylor. If you want to go north with me, there's certainly no objection on my part. But you'll have to take up the matter of expenses with the magazine. I have no authority to put you on the payroll."

She said, "Oh, I'll pay my own way. I won't even try to stick them for it. But I do want to go along." Then she smiled at me, half apologetically. "I've lived this story for months, Helm. Can you blame me for wanting to see how you handle your end of it?"

When she smiled, her face got a kind of pixie look, half wistful and half mischievous. It wasn't a bad face, as faces go. It had the proper features in the proper sizes in the proper places, and there were no visible defects or blemishes —but I did notice an odd, round little scar, relatively fresh, on her throat. Seeing this made a tingling sensation go down my spine; I had a few similar scars myself. I waited until she'd handed me my drink and turned to tap her cigarette ashes into a nearby bowl, and sure enough, on the other side and quite far back—you couldn't see how it had missed the spine—was the small exit mark.

I remembered Mac's telling me she was supposed to have been wounded. There could be little doubt of that part of the story. This girl had been shot through the neck, not too long ago, with a jacketed bullet from a military weapon. You might say she was lucky. An expanding bullet in the same place would damn near have torn her head off.

"Yes," she said, swinging back to face me abruptly,

28

"That's why I croak like a frog, Helm. Not that I ever had much of a voice."

"Sorry," I said. "Didn't mean to stare."

"I was lucky, you know," she said dryly. "I'm alive. Hal —my husband—was killed."

"Yes," I said. "I was told about that in New York." It wasn't much of a lie. At this distance, the four hundred miles separating New York from Washington dwindled to insignificance.

"One of those damn little machine pistols," she said. "It must have been nice being a foreign correspondent back in the old days when sentries had nothing but bolt-action rifles and you could run a long way between shots. We were over in East Germany. Hal had wangled it somehow; he was a great wangler. He was on the track of a story, or the follow-up of a story—maybe they told you about that at the magazine, too. He did quite a bit of work for them, from time to time. That's why I submitted my piece there. Anyway, the man at the barricade signaled us to stop, looked at the license plate, and cut loose without a word. Hal saw it coming and threw himself on top of me, so I just got the one bullet. . . . It was a deplorable accident, of course. The sentry had been drinking and the weapon was defective and ran wild when he brushed the trigger by mistake—and everybody was just as sorry as they could be, in several languages." She made a face. "The fact is that Hal was on to something, or somebody, so they got him. They let me go only after they'd made sure he hadn't told me anything of real importance."

"Somebody?" I said, keeping my voice casual. "Who?"

"A man named Caselius," she said, readily enough. " 'The Man Nobody Knows,' to quote the title of my husband's last published work—not exactly original with him, I'm afraid. The master spy of the Kremlin, if you believe in that sort of stuff. You'd be surprised how many supposedly intelligent people seem to. At least they use the word 'intelligence' in describing their activities. I may be slightly prejudiced, but I don't think it fits very well."

I said, "You sound bitter."

"You'd be bitter, too, if. . . . Look, I've lost my husband and I've barely recovered from this—" she touched her throat— "and all I want is to be left alone, and instead I can't move for falling over these creeps. I've been ques-

29

tioned till I'm ready to vomit. Where did Hal get his information about this Caselius character? Why was I kept so long in the hospital over there? Why was Hal's body cremated? Did I really see him dead. . . . *See him?*" she breathed. "I was on the floor of the car, strangling on my own blood, feeling the bullets smash into him as he shielded me. . . ."

She shivered, drew a long breath, then let her glance drop to the camera suspended from my shoulder, and spoke in a totally different tone of voice. "I certainly hope that little thing isn't what you're planning to work with when we get up to Kiruna."

I said, "That and three others like it."

"Dear God," she said flatly, "I ask for an industrial photographer, and they send me a cowboy with a candid camera!"

I looked at her for a moment, and grinned. "Don't take it out on me just because you've been heckled by a bunch of morons. And don't squawk about the pix until you've seen the proofs."

She said, still sharply, "I did get some money out of it, insurance and compensation and stuff, but Hal was kind of casual about paying his debts and I had to clean up after him. I want this story to be good enough so they'll let me do another one. Frankly, Helm, I need the dough."

"Who doesn't?" I said. "Have you got anything to wear besides those pants?"

She glanced down. "What's wrong with my pants?"

I said, "I'd rather not say. But if you've got a dress around the place, I'll buy you a dinner. Pick a restaurant that's got some light, and bring a copy of your article. The one I read in New York I had to give back to the editor."

She hesitated, and looked me over from head to foot, and smiled faintly. "I've got a dress," she said. "Have you got a dark suit, a white shirt, and a tie? They don't go in for sports clothes much here in Stockholm."

"Sounds almost like dressing for a funeral," I said. "Do I got to wear shoes, too, ma'am, or is it okay if I come barefoot?"

She looked a little startled; then she laughed. When she laughed she was quite a good-looking girl, in spite of the pants and whacked-off hair.

30

Chapter Six

I BROUGHT her back to the hotel a little before ten, took her as far as the door of her room, and put the manuscript, which I was carrying, into her hands.

"Well, I think we've got it pretty well worked out, at least for the first couple of days," I said. "Now all we have to do is shoot it. Good night, Lou."

A hint of surprise showed in her eyes. She'd obviously been prepared to put up at least a token resistance to a token pass. For me not to test her defenses at all was disconcerting. Well, that was a good way to leave her: disconcerted.

"The plane leaves at ten," I said. "I've got some errands to run in the morning, so I'll just meet you at the airport, if it's all right with you." I smiled down at her innocently from my six feet four. "I didn't know I was going to have company on this jaunt or I'd have planned it differently. But I guess you can find your own way out there."

"I'll manage," she said, a little stiffly. "It's perfectly all right. Don't worry about me. Hal trained me well. I won't be any trouble to you. I may even be some help, since I know the country and the people you'll be dealing with. Good night, Matt."

I watched her unlock the door. She didn't look bad at all. I'd been afraid, from the outfit in which she'd greeted me, that she'd turn out to be one of the dirndl girls—at least that was what those peasant costumes used to be called, I think. Maybe they've got a new name for them now: the ones that went with bare legs and thong sandals and artsy conversations.

However, she'd surprised me by appearing in a simple, long-sleeved cocktail dress of thin wool jersey—if that's the proper name for that clinging, knitted-looking material—dead black and quite plain except for a shiny black satin sash or belt done up in a kind of large bow or knot at her hip. Architecturally speaking, she wasn't exactly from Sexville, as the cats back home would put it. But the smoothly fitting black dress indicated that she wasn't hopelessly deformed, either, while at the same time it gave her a nice, smart, covered-up look that went well with her clipped, brushed hair.

She gave me a final glance and a brief smile and vanished from sight. I hoped she was feeling slightly disappointed, even if she was a respectable widow determined to be loyal to the memory of her dead husband. If I'd given her a chance to rebuff me, even in a gentle and friendly way, the advantage would have been hers. Now it was mine. I'd probably have worked it this way, being a diabolical soul, even if I hadn't had a date in the park.

Back in my room, I changed into slacks and a loose sports jacket that gave me a little more freedom than my Sunday suit. Then I opened my suitcase and took out the Smith and Wesson revolver. Mac had wanted to fit me out with some cute luggage lousy with secret compartments, but I'd pointed out that this, if discovered, would be a dead giveaway, whereas anybody who wore hats and boots like mine could probably get away with having a six-shooter —a five-shooter, to be exact—rolled up in the top of a pair of pajamas. If my stuff was examined, it would just go with my gaudy Western character.

I held the weapon for a moment, weighing it in my hand. It was compact and powerful and deadly. The hammer was shrouded so there was nothing to catch in your pocket; a low, grooved cocking piece let you shoot single-action when accuracy was important and you had the time. Not that it would ever qualify as a target pistol. I didn't like it much. It was too much cartridge for too little gun. It was an ugly, sawed-off little beast, it kicked like a mule, and when it was fired indoors the muzzle blast from the two-inch barrel sounded like an atomic explosion.

The last time I'd worked for Mac there had been a war on, and we'd been allowed to pick our own weapons. For firepower, I'd used a quiet, accurate little .22 and got along fine. But everybody was regulation-happy these peaceful days, and current armaments regulations for people in my category specified a cartridge of no less authority than a .38 Special, a requirement they'd probably got from listening to

32

some cop, since it's standard for most police departments. Of course, we weren't cops—quite the contrary—but that thought wouldn't cross the bureaucratic mind.

I rolled the little monster up in my pajama top again and tucked it back into its nest. Even if I'd liked it, tonight wasn't the time to wear it.

I took the knife from my pocket, next. It looked like an ordinary jackknife with a stag handle, except that it was just a little bigger. It wasn't in the regulations. The sections dealing with lethal cutlery were even more ridiculous and impractical than those dealing with firearms, so I'd decided to ignore them. What I had was a folding hunting knife of German Solingen steel. There were two blades, a corkscrew, and no tricks except that when the large blade was opened it locked into place, so it couldn't close accidentally on your fingers, no matter what resistance it met in dressing out game—or in any other occupation you might find for it. I'd got it from the pocket of a Nazi officer after my own knife had jammed and broken between his ribs and my partner of the moment—a girl named Tina—had had to save the situation with the butt of a gun.

It wasn't as big as a fighting knife ought to be, by a long shot, and it wasn't worth a damn for throwing, being balanced all wrong. But it was inconspicuous enough so that I could carry it anywhere, and even be seen paring my fingernails with it, without attracting much attention except for my bad manners. I'd carried it through the last year of the war, and through fifteen years of peaceful, married, law-abiding existence, when I never touched another weapon but still couldn't quite bring myself to go totally unarmed. I'd never had occasion to use it, as the saying goes, in anger. Well, there was always a first time, but that time wasn't tonight. *No weapons except in a clear and deadly emergency,* Mac had said.

I made a face at the dresser mirror. I was just teasing myself. I put the knife in a drawer and temptation behind me. It wasn't that I didn't trust my attractive, blue-haired, female *compadre,* you understand, as much as I'd trust anybody on a job like this. I'd done some checking with official sources while I was supposed to be changing for dinner; and she was the right girl, all right, operating from the right place: an exclusive little shop called Sara's Modes.

33

She had a perfect record in attendance and deportment, and she'd been thoroughly examined by her department for loyalty and right thinking: she was certified pure. The fact that she'd blown my cover within five minutes of my landing was undoubtedly a clumsy accident due to over-eagerness. I was willing to give her the benefit of the doubt. But a man with my background can't help having a certain feeling about an assignation that puts him in a lighted phone booth in a deserted park in a foreign city in the middle of the night. . . .

I had no trouble at all in finding the booth. It shone like a Christmas tree, at the edge of a little open area that ran down to the water to join the concrete promenade along the sea wall. There was grass for the kids to play on and benches for watching parents and nursemaids, but the place was empty now.

A little farther on, I saw, the sea wall ended and the walk continued along the low shore. I could see parts of the city across the water, and the lights were reflected by the smooth black surface that was broken here and there by an eddy of current—a reminder that this was, after all, a river of sorts, not a stagnant harbor or lake. There's no tide to speak of on this coast of Sweden, but the fresh waters of Lake Mälaren, west of Stockholm, flow through the city by various channels to mingle with the salt waters of the Baltic Sea, to the east.

So much I'd learned from recent reading. It seemed like a swell place to dispose of a dead body, except that the corpse would probably wash up on one of the multitudinous rocky islands of the well-known Stockholm archipelago to seaward, or be hauled up in some Scandinavian fisherman's net in an advanced state of decomposition. . . . Sometimes I think I have too much imagination for this kind of work.

I looked at the brightly lighted telephone booth. There were a number of ways I could have approached it, but only one that fitted the part I was playing. I made a smart left turn and marched up to it. Nothing happened. There was no sign or sound of anybody around. The traffic of the city was a distant murmur through the trees of the park.

I got inside the booth and, to be doing something, got out my notebook and looked up the number of the man who was arranging the hunting trips that were my excuse for bringing a rifle and a shotgun into the country. It cost me several small coins to discover that in a Swedish pay phone you deposit your money before you pick up the receiver. After I figured this out, and dialed the number, I got a peculiar signal I didn't recognize. Apparently the phones in this country played different tunes from the ones back home. The hotel switchboard must have shielded me from the shock of making this discovery earlier in the day.

While I listened, wondering what this un-American instrument would think of next, someone knocked gently on the door of the booth.

Chapter Seven

I SIGHED, hung up the phone, turned, took another deep breath, and pushed the door open. Sara Lundgren was standing there. You couldn't make out the unorthodox color of her hair in the dim light. It just looked soft and bright under her little tweed hat. She looked rather pretty and feminine to me now, after an evening in the company of the taut, shorn, dark leanness of Lou Taylor. I suppose the fact that I hadn't been quite sure I wasn't opening the door to violence, or even death, also tended to operate in her favor.

"All clear?" I asked. My voice was steady enough, I was glad to hear.

She nodded. "As far as I can tell. My car is parked on the other side of the trees. We can sit there and talk."

I don't like parked cars any more than I like phone booths. All it takes is a small amount of explosive, properly activated, or a single burst from an automatic weapon. There's no place you can go that can't be predicted and covered beforehand. But I was just a hick photographer, or, on a different level, a superannuated retread reluctantly put back into service; I wasn't supposed to be thinking of such things.

"You took your time with dinner," Sara said, guiding me into a path I hadn't seen in the dark. Her heels made small clicking sounds against the invisible pavement. "Did you have to let the woman tell you the whole story of her life? Or tell her the whole of yours? At least you could have refrained from spending an hour over the brandy! You might have realized, if you'd bothered to think, that I haven't had my clothes off since I started for Gothenburg at midnight last night!"

It was kind of like being married again, although Beth had never been the nagging type. I found myself wondering how Beth and the kids were getting on in Reno. It wasn't

36

much of a place for kids. I said, "You didn't have to follow us. You knew we'd be coming back to the hotel."

Sara said irritably, "How do you know what I have to do? Any more than I know what you have to do. All I know is that I'm supposed to watch out for you while you're here, at the request of your superiors, confirmed by mine. When *I* get an order, I obey it!"

I listened to her sharp voice, and the rapping of her smart, slim, pointed little heels, and subtracted these sounds from the total sounds of the night. I subtracted the distant traffic murmurs and the soft whisper of a vagrant breeze. That still left a little more sound than there should have been. It wasn't anything as definite as a cracking branch or even a rustling leaf. It was just the old hunter's instinct warning me that we shared this park with someone, or something.

Sara stopped abruptly. "Did you hear something? I thought I did."

"No," I said. "I didn't hear anything."

She laughed uneasily. "When I'm tired, I get nervous. I've just got the wind up a bit, I guess. Heavens, I've been overseas so long I'm beginning to talk like a Britisher! Come on."

The car was a little Kharmann-Ghia, a Volkswagen with sex appeal. It was the only vehicle in the parking area, which was located just off a wide street carrying considerable traffic, even at this hour of the night. I hadn't realized civilization was so close. As I watched, a motor scooter went past. A boy was driving, and a girl, nicely dressed, her skirt rippling in the wind of their motion, was perched gracefully sideways on the rear cushion: two kids on a date. I could imagine the scornful reaction of an American girl offered this breezy transportation after dolling herself up in high heels, nylons, and little white gloves. Behind me, the park was silent. Whoever was there was no longer moving around. Well, neither were we.

"Come on, get in!" Sara said impatiently. She had already seated herself behind the wheel.

I got into the vacant bucket seat, and closed the car door. It closed smoothly and heavily, like a trap springing shut. She was lighting a cigarette. The flame of the match brought her face out of the darkness, ghostly and surprisingly beautiful. It was hard to listen to her, when you couldn't see her, and remember that she was really a very

37

handsome woman. It was too bad she had to sound like a shrew.

"Have one?" she asked, offering me the package, perhaps as a gesture of peace.

I shook my head. "I quit. It was too much of a nuisance around the darkroom. You can't make a really sharp projection print in a room full of smoke."

She said, with a short laugh, "Don't waste that photographic line on me, my friend."

I said, "It just happens to be the truth. I've actually taken a few pictures in my life; that's why I was picked for this job, remember?"

She asked, "Well, what did you learn tonight?"

"She's coming to Kiruna with me. She wants to watch the genius at work and make sure he remembers to put film in the camera, or something. We didn't go into her motives in detail." After a moment I asked, "Who's Wellington?"

"Who?"

"Jim Wellington. A visitor to her room, apparently not for the first time. He seemed quite at home. A big man with curly hair. Just an acquaintance, she says. She also says he's kind of nice."

"American?"

"Or a reasonable facsimile. He mentioned the Baltimore Camera Club, giving the impression he'd once been a star member."

"I'll put through a query," Sara said. She took out a notebook, turned it to face the street lights, and wrote. "Wellington. . . . Description?"

I gave it to her. "He's supposed to represent some U.S. plastics firm," I said.

"Anything else to add about him?"

I shook my head. "No."

That Jim Wellington had been a member of one of our undercover units during the war, and had made a flight across the Channel from a certain field in England on a certain date, was information I was keeping to myself for a while. Not that it labeled him, necessarily, as an honest and upright citizen; a lot of men who'd risked their necks for democracy back in those days had turned their reckless courage and their wartime training into less creditable and more lucrative channels since. But it was something I had on the man that, probably, nobody else around here had;

and I wasn't going to toss it into the common pool of knowledge until I was quite sure I had no use for it myself. Anyway, he'd kept his mouth shut about me. I could do the same for him until I saw a good reason not to.

"Anything else about the woman?" Sara asked.

I shook my head again. "Not much. She's very good as the grieving widow, bitter but helpless to exact vengeance, now striking out bravely to build a literary career of her own. What do you people have on her?"

Sara said: "What we've got is this: their Peugeot sedan was thoroughly riddled with bullets. We were shown the car afterwards. There were lots of holes. They were real holes; you could see daylight through them. There was lots of blood. It was human blood; that was checked. An urn of ashes was buried later. It was inconvenient to analyze them, and it wouldn't have proved anything, anyway. The people we're dealing with can procure a human body to burn if they want one, and I suppose one body has about the same inorganic composition as another. The widow attended the ceremony with a bandage around her neck and tears in her eyes. The bandage was real and covered a real wound; our witness didn't vouch for the tears. And the fact remains that Harold Taylor disappeared at a time when a lot of our people were looking for him to ask him a lot of questions—disappeared from a place he wasn't supposed to be, a place he could only have reached with a lot of co-operation from the other side."

I asked, "How much of the stuff in his article checks out?"

The woman beside me laughed shortly and blew smoke against the windshield. I have nothing, in principle, against women smoking, but since I've quit myself I must say I find the odor of perfume more attractive than that of tobacco.

She said, "What is there to check against, Helm? He describes Caselius as a big man with a beard; a Cossack type with a great rumbling laugh. It sounds unlikely on the face of it—it's a much too conspicuous appearance for a man engaged in secret work—but it could be a disguise Caselius affects on occasion. Anyway, it's the only description we have, so we can't argue with it. Taylor describes the organization. It's their standard organizational setup, so he's probably fairly close there. He describes several typical operations. Some are on record. He could have learned about them at our end. The information's supposed to be confidential, of course, but he had the reputation of being very persuasive. Other operations, there's no way of checking. If somebody photographed a certain secret document, returned it to its proper place in the files, and sent the negative to Caselius, how can we know until the stuff is used against us?"

I asked, "Is there any possibility that Taylor himself is Caselius, and took this way of getting out from under?"

Sara glanced at me sharply. "Where did you get that idea? Did the woman say anything—"

I kicked myself, mentally. I should have remembered that I was dealing with the intelligence mind, and kept my trap shut. To an intelligence agent, there's no such thing as somebody figuring something out for himself. The information must have been leaked to him by somebody else— preferably somebody who wasn't supposed to have talked and must be identified and punished. In this respect, the intelligence mind is indistinguishable from the security mind. When dealing with either intelligence or security people, there's only one motto to follow: don't be bright, they don't recognize the existence of brains.

"She didn't have to say anything," I said. "It's a fairly obvious gimmick, isn't it?"

Sara said, rather stiffly, "I don't know how obvious it is. We have considered the theory, of course, and it's very interesting that you should mention it right after having a long conversation with. . . . You're sure Mrs. Taylor didn't suggest it to you in some way, maybe quite indirectly?"

"Quite sure," I said. "I dreamed it up all by myself."

"Well," she said, still dissatisfied, "well, we don't take it too seriously, but we are checking his movements over the past several years and seeing if there's any correlation with what we know of Caselius' operations. Taylor did move around a great deal, doing articles for various publications, and as a prominent American journalist he had contacts everywhere. There's a lot of hate-America propaganda these days, you know; but there are also a lot of government officials in a lot of countries who'll tell an American things they wouldn't tell anybody else. Generally they've got an ax of some kind to grind, and hope Uncle Sam will supply the whetstone, given the right kind of publicity. Taylor was a genius at sniffing out these people, apparently. And he was also, I gather, the kind of flamboyant character who'd get a big kick out of writing himself up as a master spy, complete with Cossack beard and rumbling laugh, and collecting money for the piece, just before he pretended to be killed and took refuge on the other side of the iron curtain. He had that kind of a sense of humor, they say."

Her voice was disapproving. Obviously she didn't like flamboyant humorists.

I said, "Of course, he doesn't have to *be* Caselius. He could just have been working for the man and decided that things were getting too hot for him and it was time to run to the boss for shelter. But could he have carried it off for years without his wife's knowing about it?"

Sara said, "It seems unlikely, doesn't it? However, she *was* shot, apparently. We don't really know how well the Taylor family got along. Men have been known to get tired of their wives, particularly if the wives happened to learn too much about them."

"She's under the impression he saved her life," I said. "Or says she is, which may only mean that one of them is a hell of a good actor. Well, let's sum it up. We can take the Taylor article two ways. One, it's the straight dope, and Taylor just learned too much for his own good, somehow, and made the mistake of publishing it. So he was lured into a deadfall and killed to keep him from spilling whatever else he might have found out that he hadn't put in this article and might put in the next. His wife happened to survive, and was released after they'd observed her long enough to be pretty sure she didn't know enough to do any damage."

"Yes," Sara said. "It could be that way. In which case you're wasting your time with her."

I said, "She's a bright girl; I've wasted more time in worse company." The woman beside me stirred; perhaps she took the remark personally. I went on crisply: "The other possibility is that Taylor is either Caselius or is working for him, and the article was just a kind of smokescreen he threw out when it was decided that the time had come for the character of Harold Taylor, American journalist, to be dramatically withdrawn from circulation. In this case, of course, the article isn't worth the paper it's written on. What about the wife? Did he try to kill her to shut her up, or was there perhaps a lot of shooting to make his so-called death look plausible to her, in the midst of which she took a bullet accidentally? In that case, she's still innocent, and we're still wasting time playing with her. Or is she in cahoots with him, an accomplice sent back to serve some sinister purpose, now that he no longer dares show himself in his old haunts? In that case, explain her wound."

"Plastic surgery," Sara said.

"She'd have to love the guy a lot to let herself in for spending the rest of her life with a scarred neck and a baritone voice."

"Maybe the surgeons promised to make her as good as new when the job is done, whatever it is," Sara said. "Anyway, women do strange things for men."

"And men for women," I said, "and so endeth our philosophy lesson for the day, inconclusively. Are there any final remarks you'd care to add before we adjourn the meeting?"

She shook her head. "No," she said, and hesitated. "No, but. . . . Helm?"

"Yes?"

"If you find Caselius. . . ." Her voice trailed off.

"Yes?"

She drew a deep breath and turned to face me. "Before you . . . before I help you any further, I must know what you intend to do. Are you going to try to smuggle him back to the States as a prisoner, or will you just turn him over to the Swedish authorities?"

I glanced at her, a little surprised. "Honey," I said, "that's none of your damn business. I have my orders. Let it go at that." Then I frowned. "What do you care? Do you have a yen for this mystery man?"

She drew herself up haughtily. "Don't be vulgar! But—"

"Quite apart from his value to the other side," I said, "which I've heard estimated at a couple of armored divisions or the equivalent in fully equipped missile bases, you said yourself he's responsible for several deaths among your colleagues, in addition to what may or may not have happened to Harold Taylor."

She said coldly, "I'm not responsible for Caselius' conscience, Helm. I am responsible for my own."

I said, "Okay, honey. Spell it out."

"You've been sent to kill him, haven't you? That's your job, to hunt down a human being like an animal and destroy him! And I'm supposed to . . . to assist you in accomplishing your mission!"

"Go on," I said, as she hesitated.

She said, "I'm in *intelligence*, Mr. Helm. I'm a spy, if you like, and it's not a very respectable profession, I'll admit, but my job is to collect and evaluate information. It is *not* to act as a hound dog for a hunter of men! Not that you look to me like a very efficient hunter, but that's neither here nor there. The fact is. . . ." The ash from her cigarette dropped into her lap, and she brushed at it quickly, annoyed by the distraction, and returned her attention to me. "There's a man called Mac, isn't there? And there's an organization that hasn't got a name, but they call it the wrecking crew, or sometimes the M-group. The M stands for murder, Helm!"

I hadn't heard that one. Some smart-alec must have come up with it since my time. "You're telling it, honey," I said. "Keep it coming."

Her head came up sharply. "Damn you, don't call me honey! Do you know where I got this information? Not from our side, from theirs! For years we've been hearing sly propaganda about an American *Mordgruppe*—hearing it and laughing at it and combating it as best we could, thinking it was nothing but their clumsy effort to justify their own dirty assassination teams. I can remember, when I was stationed in Paris, laughing myself silly when somebody asked me in all seriousness about this fellow called Mac, in Washington, who points a finger and someone dies. 'My *dear man*,' I said, giggling, *'you can't really believe we operate like that!'* But we do, don't we?"

I said, "Finish the story, Sara. Let's pass the rhetorical questions."

She said, "I knew there was something odd when we were notified you were coming. . . . Helm, don't we *stand* for anything? Have they actually succeeded in dragging us down to their level? Is the world simply divided into two hostile camps, with no moral distinction between them? I had to have a look at you; that's why I went to Gothenburg this morning, even though it was terribly bad technique. I had to see what kind of a man. . . . I'm not going to do it, Helm! I've given you all the help you're going to get. As a matter of fact—"

"As a matter of fact, what?"

"Never mind," she said. "You can protest through channels, of course. You can try to have me removed from my post."

43

"Don't worry," I said. I reached for the door handle. "Don't worry about a thing, Sara. Just go back to collecting and evaluating important information. . . . Well, I'd better be getting back to the hotel, and I guess I'd better arrive on foot, since I left that way."

She said, "Helm, I—"

"What?"

"Don't sneer just because I—"

"No sneer was intended, honey. I respect all your finer feelings, every last little one of them."

"Can't you understand how I feel? Can't I make you see how *wrong* it is?"

My wife had asked me that, too. She'd wanted me to understand how she felt, and I'd understood perfectly. She'd wanted me to see how wrong it was, and I'd seen. They all see what's wrong with the world, and tell you all about it —as if you'd never noticed it before—but none of them has any practical suggestions about how to fix it. One day we'll all live on chemicals and never kill a living thing. Meanwhile, we eat meat and take the world as it is. At least some of us do.

"Good night, Sara," I said, getting out of the car.

Walking away, I was aware of a quick, glowing arc at the corner of my vision as she flicked her cigarette away into the dark. The car door slammed shut behind me. The little Volkswagen motor in the tail of the Ghia started to turn over, and stopped abruptly. I heard her muffled cry. Then they were on top of me.

Lead with your right and take your licking like a man, Mac had said, but it was a good thing I'd taken the precaution of leaving the knife behind. It was a wonderful, tempting spot for it. There's nothing like a knife when you're outnumbered three to one and fighting in the dark. But I didn't have it, and I wasn't supposed to know judo or karate, and as far as I'm concerned fist fighting is for kids. I did get one of them lightly with my knee, hoping it would seem accidental, and I bruised my knuckles on the other two, swinging wildly.

Then they had me by the arms, and a couple more were shoving Sara Lundgren along the walk toward me.

Chapter Eight

THEY TOOK us back through the trees into the little clearing where there was some illumination from the gaudy phone booth, from the lights along the sea-wall promenade, and from the open sky that had the faint yellow glow that goes with any big city, anywhere in the world. The stars looked weak and far away. They'd been much closer, I remembered, back home in New Mexico.

I wasn't really scared, however. We were over the first hurdle. If killing had been on the program, I figured, I'd have been dead already. That had been the greatest risk, considering the circumstances, and it was past. Now we were playing games. All I had to do was keep the rules clearly in mind, and I'd be all right. Well, relatively all right. I don't suppose any normal man really enjoys being beat up.

The three of them went to work on me again. They were quite amateurish about it. I got pummeled here and there, I got a cut lip and that would probably turn into a black eye, and a hole in the knee of my slacks when I went down. I was glad I'd had the forethought to change from my good suit. Each one of my attackers was very careful to offer himself to me, wide open, every time he came in to take his swing. You had to hand it to them. They were brave men. They exposed themselves to kicks that would have maimed them for life, to blows that would have killed them—and every time I managed to break free I'd put my head down and charge in swinging like the hero of a TV saloon brawl, and they'd all pile on top of me, and we'd start all over again.

I caught glimpses of Sara between her two guards, first struggling and calling my name and pleading with them to stop, then standing breathless and defeated, and finally, woman-like, beginning to tuck herself in and button herself up and smooth herself down mechanically even as she continued to watch the proceedings with fear and horror. It took me a while to locate the sniper. Finally I caught a glimpse of him among the trees beyond the phone booth, a dark shadow holding a weapon that gleamed dully as he watched my performance, no doubt, with a critical eye.

It's a foregone conclusion that they're going to test you out carefully before they accept you as harmless, Mac had said, and now I was undergoing my entrance exams. The surprising, and encouraging, thing was that they'd still bother. Even if they'd had no evidence against me before, which wasn't likely, just catching me here with Sara, the local undercover representative of Uncle Sam, was enough to tell them all they needed to know about me. As a stupid free-lance photographer, I was totally unmasked. But it seemed as if I might still be able to do business as a stupid intelligence agent, a thing I'd barely dared hope for, although Mac had obviously had it in mind when he arranged my advance publicity. Apparently these people needed me for something. Otherwise, why hadn't they either killed me or simply ignored me?

But they checked me out thoroughly. That was, of course, why I'd been hauled out here where there was some light to see by—to shoot by, if necessary. I was to be knocked around, humiliated, goaded beyond endurance, in the hope that if I was putting on an act I could be made to lose my temper and reveal myself as something more dangerous than I seemed. In that case, presumably, my attackers would dive for cover and the man among the trees would take care of things permanently with the chopper he held.

They were treating me to choice insults in Swedish now, testing my linguistic abilities, as we milled around flailing at each other breathlessly. At least the words I recognized weren't very nice. However, you have to know a language very well to appreciate its more esoteric blasphemies. These weren't expressions I'd normally have encountered as a nice little boy in Minnesota, and they hadn't been on the vocabulary lists I'd had to memorize more recently, either, although you'd think a practical language course would give some attention to such details. . . .

Suddenly it was over, and they were just hanging onto me. Dead game to the end, as the British would say, I threw myself around some more and tried to jerk my arms free and ignored an invitation to break the shin of the guy to my right with the hard heel of my shoe.

"You bastards," I gasped, "you yellow bastards, what the hell do you think you're doing, anyway? I'm an American citizen—" Well, you can fill in the rest of my angry monologue for yourself. I take no pride in it. At last my breath ran out and we all stood there panting.

The man among the trees spoke. *"Försök med kvinna,"* he said.

I jerked around to look at him, as if aware of his presence for the first time. What he'd said was, *"Try with the woman."* It was time to toss them a bone, and I gasped, "You leave her alone, whoever you are! She's got nothing to do with—"

"With what, Mr. Helm? With taking innocent photographs for American publications?" The sniper laughed. "Please, Mr. Helm! Give us credit. We know who she is. And we know who you are, and why you're here. . . . So you *do* understand some Swedish, after all?"

I said angrily, "You think you're pretty smart, don't you? So help me, if I get my hands on you—"

The man to my left hit me across the mouth. The man in the trees said, "Not likely, Mr. Helm. Not even though I understand you've come a long way to find me. I assure you, if you did get your clumsy hands on Caselius, it would do you very little good. Quite the contrary, in fact."

It was my cue to struggle madly to break free and reach him, although just what I expected to accomplish bare-handed against his machine pistol wasn't quite clear. But it was good TV stuff and it went over big. Actually, I hadn't the slightest hope of getting near him tonight, and I didn't even intend to make a serious attempt. For one thing, I had no assurance that the man among the trees was really the man I wanted, and I wasn't going to get myself killed or badly hurt trying for a decoy.

"You wait!" I cried, allowing myself to be subdued. "You just wait, Mister Caselius! It's your trick tonight, but you'd better stop horsing around now and kill me, or some day when you haven't got that gun and an army to help you—"

One of them clipped me alongside the head. The sniper in the trees snapped an order in a language I didn't understand. One man detached himself from the group about me,

47

leaving two holding me. The single man started toward Sara, who drew back apprehensively, but was seized again by the two men flanking her. As the lone man approached, the other two gave her a sudden shove, propelling her toward the third. He stepped quickly aside and thrust out a foot, so that she tripped and hit the grass full length, with a nice display of legs and lingerie. I shouted something incoherent and appropriate and, lunging free—they made it easy for me this time—charged in to protect her from further abuse.

Two men came to meet me, offering the usual opportunities for scientific mayhem, which I ignored, sticking to my windmill, wild-western attack. I suppose there are people who can accomplish something with their fists—Joe Louis for one—but I'd as soon go into a brawl armed with nothing but a fresh-baked roll and a well-done hamburger. You can't do any real, disabling damage with a fist—at least I can't—and when you hit a guy with one, damn it, it hurts. But I was a red-blooded, fist-fighting American boy tonight, and we had a fine slugging match over and around the prostrate form of Sara Lundgren. In the middle of it she scrambled to her feet and tried to run, limping from the loss of one of her high-heeled pumps, only to be caught by a man waiting outside the meleé.

They got me pinioned again—it took two of them to hold me; I was a real tiger that night—and Sara's captor sent her stumbling into the arms of the other two, who tossed her right back at him. He missed the catch, and she tripped on the edge of the walk and sat down hard on the unyielding pavement. They were laughing now, jeering at me and challenging me to come to her aid as they picked her up and passed her back and forth some more before dumping her again, sobbing and disheveled, at my feet.

I struggled with the men who held me. I cursed them in English and dipped into border Spanish. I threw some of their Swedish expressions back at them. Then I went back to my wartime French and German for some really descriptive terminology. I was giving myself away badly now. As a hick photographer, I wasn't supposed to know all these languages. But my cover was shot to hell, anyway, and the dreadful spectacle before me was driving me mad. . . .

Actually, of course, the woman was nothing to me. I owed her nothing; I had no reason to be fond of her, and some to dislike her. Oh, if I'd thought she was likely to

48

wind up crippled or disfigured or dead, it would have been different. But we were still playing games, and it was obviously just a mussing-up job like I'd got myself—gentler, if anything. They were shoving her around a lot, and it looked brutal, but I noticed that nobody'd really hauled off and hit her—and between bouts of swearing and struggling I watched her disintegration with clinical interest and, I suspect, a trace of mean satisfaction.

I mean, these righteous people give me a pain, anyway; and while a shabby, humble martyr can be quite admirable in adversity, there's always something a little comical about a proud and well-dressed idealist caught off base. To watch Sara Lundgren, the fastidious morality kid who'd have no truck with violence—hatless and shoeless now, grass-stained and dirty, with her expensive suit popping its buttons and bursting its seams and her skinned knees emerging through her ripped stockings—to watch her pantingly trying to evade her male tormentors didn't arouse in me much feeling of pity or indignation, particularly since I was fairly sure she'd helped plan the evening's entertainment herself.

As I said earlier, after checking I'd been prepared to trust her as much as anybody, but on a job like this I don't trust anybody much. She'd pointed me out by trailing me across the country. She was the one who'd arranged for us to meet here; and she'd given the close-in signal with her cigarette when I started to leave. For an attractive and well-dressed woman deliberately to arrange for her own transformation into a female scarecrow seemed fairly cold-blooded, to be sure; but having fingered me, she'd naturally want to stage a very plausible scene to allay my suspicions.

I didn't know her motives, but she'd undoubtedly convinced herself it was for the good of mankind—they all do, ever since Judas caught hell for doing it for cash—and all it was really costing her was a few scratches and bruises, a little dignity, and a fall outfit she'd probably got at a discount through her own dress shop. . . .

It stopped with a single word from the man among the trees, in the language I didn't know. The three men stepped back, leaving Sara sprawled on the grass where she'd last been spilled, crying weakly, a dramatic figure of exhaustion and despair. Her clothing seemed to have divided itself into two parts, bunched about her hips and armpits, so that she looked half naked lying there, and suddenly her dishevelment wasn't funny any longer. She was a woman and we were men, and I wished she'd stop the foolishness and sit up, button her damn blouse and jacket, and pull her damn skirt down where it belonged.

The man among the trees spoke another command. I was dragged back a couple of steps by the men who held me; and the ones out in the open hurried toward us. Sara stopped crying and scrambled to her feet, so quickly that even if I'd never had a suspicion of her, I'd have known then that the whole act was phony.

"No," she said.

She was looking toward the trees. Everything had changed. We'd had a lot of fun kidding each other and knocking each other around playfully, but you can't play games forever. You've got to grow up some time.

I became aware again of the distant murmur of Stockholm traffic. The stars seemed farther away than ever. The slender woman in the center of the open space made a hasty, breathless, very feminine gesture toward pushing back her disordered hair and smoothing down her ruined clothes; she moved in stocking feet toward the shadow in the woods, her hands outstretched pleadingly.

"*No,*" she gasped. "*Please . . . no! You can't!*"

The weapon answered her.

Chapter Nine

As THE GUN went off, I threw myself flat, tearing myself loose from the men who held me. There was nothing I could do for her. He wouldn't miss at that range. I fully expected to be the next target. I rolled toward one of the park benches for such shelter as it could give. No bullets came near me. Presently I sat up, foolish and alone except for the still figure on the grass. Everyone else had departed the scene.

There had been no gaudy farewell speeches, no threats or promises, no blood-curdling ultimatums, just that single, short, accurate burst of automatic fire and some quick footsteps among the trees. I heard a car start up somewhere and drive away. I got up and walked forward. She was quite dead, of course. It was time for me to get out of there before the shooting brought the police, but I stood looking down at her for a moment. It wasn't a very nice moment.

Not that her death changed my opinion about her part in the night's events. I still thought she'd betrayed me. She'd merely been double-crossed in her turn. But that didn't matter now. What mattered was that I'd stood by, gleefully watching her being mauled and humiliated, taking satisfaction in the sight. I'd let her get my goat with her high-flown talk of murder and moral distinctions. . . .

The Stockholm police carry sabers three feet long. So help me, I saw one. They are courageous men. They'll charge into a dark wood toward the sound of submachine-gun fire, armed with nothing but a yard of cold steel. Well, the world is full of brave men. My experience has been that the cowards are in the minority. I've been brave myself upon occasion, but that night wasn't one of the occasions. There wasn't anything left to be brave about. I'd have loved to find something.

After the sword-bearing officer had run by, I slipped out

of my hiding place in the bushes and made my way back to the hotel. Various official vehicles were converging on the park. They didn't use sirens. Instead they made a kind of braying, hee-haw noise, like musical donkeys. I recalled reading somewhere that over here sirens were reserved for air raid warnings and such. It's not a bad idea, come to think of it. Back home, hearing a wailing in the distance, you never know whether you're dealing with a brush fire in a vacant lot, a kid snatching a purse, or an intercontinental missile with a hydrogen warhead zeroed in on your home town.

I made it to my room without encountering anybody who might have noticed my torn pants, my battered face, and my grim and fearsome expression—at least it felt grim and fearsome. I didn't take a drink. I didn't have anything to celebrate. I just took a hot bath and two sleeping pills, and went to bed. I was just a retread, too old to be much use. If someone wanted to kill me in my sleep, he was welcome.

I didn't sleep very well, in spite of the pills. I kept seeing a slender, disheveled woman with bright hair that looked blonde in the dusk, stretching out her hands toward a shape in the woods, pleading for mercy. Then the dream changed. I was being attacked from all sides. I was overwhelmed, pinned to the ground; they were all over me and I was being slowly smothered by the weight of them. . . . I opened my eyes abruptly to see light in the room. A man was bending over me. His hand was across my mouth.

We stared at each other in silence, our faces less than a foot apart. He was quite a handsome and distinguished-looking man, with thick, black, well-combed hair, grayed at the temples. He had a little black moustache. He hadn't been wearing a moustache when I'd seen him last, there'd been no gray in his hair, and his arm had been in a cast up to the shoulder.

"You are careless, Eric," he murmured, taking his hand away. "You sleep too heavy. And you still have bad dreams."

"I don't know why they bother with a key for this room, the way people wander in and out at will," I said. "Roll up your left sleeve."

He laughed. "Ah, we play tricks. It was the right one, don't you recall?" He started to take off his coat.

"Hi, Vance," I said. "Never mind stripping. I remember you."

I got up, shook my head to clear it, went into the bathroom and started the hot water running. I got a jar of instant coffee and a plastic cup out of my suitcase. I loaded the cup with the powder and went back to the bathroom to fill it. The water was almost hot enough. I sat down on the bed to drink, without offering any to Vance. I hadn't invited him. If he was thirsty, he could supply is own coffee, or at least his own cup.

"Don't smoke," I said to him as he produced cigarettes. "I don't, and somebody might wonder who stunk up the curtains."

He chuckled and lit the cigarette. "They will think it was just your lady friend. The one with the strange hair."

I rose and knocked the cigarette from his fingers and stepped on it. "I said don't do it!"

He looked up at me. "Careful, Eric!"

I said, "I could take you, Vance. I could always take you."

He said calmly, "It was never proved. Some time we must try. But not here and now."

I sat down on the bed again, and polished off my almost-warm-enough coffee. "Sorry, *amigo*," I said. "I've had a rough night, and nembutal makes me irritable. Furthermore, I'm not in a mood for jocular references to the lady in question. She happens to be dead."

"Dead?" He frowned quickly. "The commotion in the park?" I nodded, and he said: "At whose hands? Yours?"

"Why do you say that?"

"One of my reasons for coming was to warn you against trusting her too far. It wasn't a message we could send through her apparatus, naturally. It appears that her department is secretly investigating some derogatory reports, which they only recently got around to mentioning to us."

"I'd say the reports were probably correct," I said. "But it was our man who got her. At least he announced himself by name, and now I'm inclined to think it actually was Caselius. Unfortunately, he gave me no opportunity to look at him in the light, and I think he was disguising his voice. . . . It was a cat-and-mouse act, Vance. Kind of lousy. They let her assist at her own funeral; they let her co-operate with them in making a holy spectacle of herself; they let her think until the last moment that she was just helping them to kid me along. Then they killed her. He killed her.

"It was a great joke, and whoever set it up would have wanted to be there to laugh. That's why I think it was Caselius himself. He wouldn't have bothered to arrange all that specialized fun for another guy. He'd have wanted to be there to finish her off himself, and see the horror in her eyes as she realized how cruelly she'd been tricked." After a moment, I said, "I figure he killed her because she'd served her purpose and he couldn't leave her alive to talk. That means she had something to talk about. I've got to go on to Kiruna in the morning with the Taylor woman. Can you check on two men for me?"

"I can try."

I said, "One man I don't know. But she said she was going to be married as soon as she finished her tour of duty here; and I think the bereaved fiancé deserves a little of our attention. *Somebody* filled her full of fine ideals and used them to make a sucker of her. The other is a man who currently calls himself Jim Wellington. I have no evidence of a connection between him and Lundgren—he does know Taylor—but maybe you can find one. Watch out for him; he's been through the mill.

"He wasn't one of ours, but he made a flight with me into France from our usual field, some time in late '44 or early '45. Some of those people went bad later, and some even changed sides. He might be one of them. I don't know his outfit, but I'll give you a description and Mac can find the date I made that flight and check the official records for my companion. Tell him it was that prison-break operation at St. Alice. My job was to take the commandant out of action with a scoped-up rifle five minutes before they blew the gates. I got the damn commandant, all right, but nobody else showed up, as in most of those lousy cooperative jobs, and I had a hell of a time getting clear. . . .

"Hell, I'm talking too much. I guess I've got a bit of a jag on. She wasn't much, Vance. Just a pretty clothes horse with intellectual and moral pretensions that she didn't have the brains to live up to—just the kind who'd be a patsy for a clever character with a humanitarian spiel. But I don't like the way she died, *amigo*. I just don't like the lousy way she died!"

54

He said, "Take it easy, friend Eric. In our business, one does not work well if one lets oneself become emotionally involved."

I said, "I'll get over it. I'm just a little shook-up tonight. Somebody held up a mirror, and I didn't like the looks of the fellow inside the frame. As for that guy Caselius—"

He said, "You had better get over it. You are going to have to restrain your vengeful impulses."

"What do you mean?"

He was reaching in his coat pocket. He said, "This is ironical, Eric. It is really very ironical."

"Maybe," I said. "I can see that it's a lot of things, but I haven't spotted much irony yet."

He said, "I had another reason for coming, a direct communication from the master of ceremonies himself."

"The master of—"

He laughed. "MC," he said. "Mac. It is a joke."

"I'm not up on all the jokes yet," I said.

"This is no joke, however," he said. He gave me a folded sheet of paper. "Read it and you will see the irony, too. I could tell you the gist of it, but I will let you decipher it yourself so as not to miss the full flavor of Mac's prose."

I looked at him, and at the paper; and I took the paper to the little writing table by the wall and went to work on it. Presently I had it lying before me in plain language. It had my code number and the usual transmission signals. The station of origin was Washington, D.C. The text read:

Representations from female agent Stockholm have led to serious case of cold feet locally. Temporarily, we hope, your orders are changed as follows: you are to make firm identification of subject if possible but do not, repeat do not, carry out remainder of original instructions. Find him, keep him in sight, but don't hurt a hair of his cute little head. Realize difficulty of assignment, sympathize. Working hard to stiffen local backbones. Be ready for go-ahead signal, but under no circumstances take action unless you receive. Repeat, under no circumstances. This is an order. This is an order. Don't get independent, damn you, or we're all cooked. Love, Mac.

Chapter Ten

LOU TAYLOR was waiting impatiently when I arrived at the field in a taxi, having slept too long, after my session with Vance, to catch the official airport bus.

"I was beginning to think you weren't going to make it," she said, and gave me a second look. "My God, what happened to you?"

My cut lip didn't show up too badly, although it felt very conspicuous, and I'd hoped my sunglasses hid the shiner, but apparently not. "You won't believe it," I said, "but I ran into the closet door in the dark."

She laughed. "You were right the first time. I don't believe it."

I grinned. "All right, I'll tell you the truth. I couldn't sleep last night, so I took a walk around town, and three big bruisers came out of an alley and attacked me for no good reason. Of course, being a right-living American boy, I beat hell out of all three of them, but one got through with a lucky punch."

"A likely story!" she said. "Well, you'd better get this paraphernalia checked in; there's not much time left before takeoff. Here, I'll give you a hand."

"Take it easy with that camera bag," I said. "Drop that and we're out of business."

They don't let you take pictures from an airplane over Sweden, so I guess all the security nuts in the world don't live in New Mexico, although sometimes when I'm home it seems that way. I took the seat by the window, nevertheless; Lou said it didn't matter to her. All scenery looks just about the same from a plane, she said, and she'd already seen it twice getting the dope for her story, going and coming.

Presently the stewardess announced in Swedish and English that we were flying at nine hundred meters and would reach Luleå—pronounced Lulie-oh—in two and a half hours. Lou informed me that the reported altitude was equivalent to approximately twenty-seven hundred feet since, she said, a meter is only a little longer than a yard —thirty-nine and four-tenths inches, to be exact.

Already there were forests below us, and open fields, red roofs, plenty of lakes and streams, and more forests. I had a funny feeling of having seen it all before, although I'd never been closer to it than Britain and the continent of Europe. It was just something my romantic imagination was making up from knowing that my forebears had lived in this country a long time. I suppose a guy named Kelly would feel the same way flying over Ireland.

Then we swung out over the Gulf of Bothnia, that long finger of the Baltic that separates Sweden from Finland, and soon there was nothing to look at but water, roughened by a brisk cross wind. I turned to my companion and found that she was asleep. She looked all right that way, but at twenty-six, her age of record, she wasn't quite young enough to get sentimental about, sleeping. Only the truly young look really good asleep. They get a kind of innocence about them, no matter what kind of juvenile monsters they may be when they're awake. The rest of us haven't that much innocence left. We can be thankful if we manage to sleep with our mouths closed and don't snore.

She was wearing a brown wool skirt—kind of a pleasant rusty color—and a matching sweater with a neck high enough to cover the scar on her throat. The sweater was good wool but not cashmere; she wasn't a kid who blew her roll on clothes. Her shoes had set her back something, though. They were strong British walking shoes with sturdy soles. Although I had to respect her good sense, I must say I prefer my women in high heels. Well, at least she'd had the decency to wear nylons. If there's anything that turns my stomach, it's a grown woman in bobby sox.

I lay back in my seat beside the sleeping girl and listened to the sound of the plane's motors and let my thoughts wander. Mac's little sentence had been a classic of its kind, I reflected: *Realize difficulty of assignment, sympathize.* In effect, I was being asked to locate, identify, and keep an eye on a man-eating tiger—but under no circumstances to shoot the beast. *Repeat, under no circumstances. This is an order. This is an order.* Clearly Mac

57

was scared stiff I might try to be clever and rig up something resembling self-defense. He was in political trouble of some kind, and he didn't want any dead bodies whatever cluttering up the landscape until he got things straightened out.

Sara Lundgren had hinted that she was doing more than merely refusing to help me. What she'd meant, apparently, was that she'd lodged a stiff protest in Washington against my assignment. As Vance had said, it was ironical. I wondered how she'd have felt if she'd known that her action would prevent us, at least temporarily, from avenging her death. Of course, some of those idealists are pretty stubborn, and it was quite possible that she'd have been in favor of turning the other cheek. . . .

Mac's worst enemies had always been the gentle folks back home. As he'd said himself once during the war, there wasn't much danger of the Nazis breaking us up, but one soft-hearted U.S. Senator could do it with a few words. Nowadays it seems to be all right to plan on, and create the machines for, exterminating millions of human beings at a crack, but just to send out the guy to rub out another who's getting to be an active menace, that's still considered very immoral and reprehensible.

I'll admit that I found the idea a little startling myself, even in wartime, when Mac first explained to me exactly what this group was that I'd been picked to join. It was in that office of his in London, with a view of wrecked buildings through the single dusty window, and I'd just been through the first phase of my training—the one you got while they were still evaluating your possibilities and deciding whether they wanted you, after all. Mac had looked up at me for a moment as I stood before his desk.

"Hunter, aren't you?" he'd said, and then he'd asked me some questions about Western hunting. Finally he said, "Doesn't seem as if you're very particular about what you hunt, Lieutenant." That was before I'd been assigned the code name Eric, that had been mine ever since.

"No, sir," I said.

"Well, I think we can find you some game, if you don't mind stalking a quarry that can shoot back."

Anyway, that's approximately the way the conversation went. It's a long time ago, now, and I won't vouch for the exact words. He always did like to get men who'd done some hunting; it was the first thing he looked for in a prospective candidate. It wasn't that you couldn't train city boys to be just as efficient, as far as the mechanics of the job were concerned, he explained to me once, but they tended to lack the balance of men who were accustomed to going out once a year to shoot something specific, under definite legal restrictions. A city kid, turned loose with a gun, either took death too seriously and made a great moral issue of the whole business—and generally finished by cracking up under a load of self-imposed guilt—or, finding himself free of restraint for the first time in his life, turned into a crazy butcher.

What criterion Mac used for the women—yes, we had some then and still do—I don't know.

I've never been ashamed of it. On the other hand, I've never talked about it, if only because I was under orders not to. Even my wife, until quite recently, thought I'd spent the war at a desk, doing public relations work for the Army. When she stumbled onto the truth, she couldn't stand it. I supposed it changed her whole picture of me, herself, and our marriage. Instead of having for a husband a staid, respectable, kindly man with literary inclinations, she suddenly found herself bound to an unpredictable and potentially violent character, capable of deeds she could barely imagine.

Well, we're all capable of deeds we can barely imagine. Beth's attitude still had the power to annoy me a little, because I was quite sure she'd never have dreamed of breaking up our home if she'd merely discovered, say, that I was the bombardier who'd pushed the button over Hiroshima. I must say that I don't get it. Why honor and respect a guy who drops a great indiscriminate bomb, and recoil in horror from a guy who shoots a small, selective bullet? Sara Lundgren had had the same attitude. She'd been perfectly willing, presumably, to collect data, as part of her job, for the use of the Strategic Air Command—that might lead to the eventual obliteration of a city or two—but she'd balked violently at the idea of feeding information to a lone man with a gun.

To be perfectly honest, even before I rejoined, more or less as a reaction to Beth's leaving me, I'd always been just a little proud of having been a member of Mac's outfit. After all, it was an elite organization: the wrecking crew

59

—the *Mordgruppe,* as the Nazis had called us—the last resort of the lace-pants boys. When they came up against someone too tough for them to handle, they called on us. The M-Group....

Lou Taylor awoke when we landed at Luleå. There were gray-green military planes on the field marked with three gold crowns, presumably the insignia of the Swedish air force. From Luleå, the airlines map showed, we had to make a hitch due west first, before bearing up to the northwest for Kiruna. I asked the stewardess about this when we were airborne again, and was told that we had to make a little detour because the Swedish Army didn't like people flying over its great fortress at Boden. It was the first I'd heard of it, and I couldn't help wondering what a fortress looked like these atomic days, and who was kidding whom.

Soon the stewardess announced that we were crossing the Arctic Circle; shortly thereafter she came to the seat and pointed out to us—I guess we looked like tourists—an impressive, snowcapped mountain range ahead, the backbone of the Scandinavian peninsula. Beyond was Norway. Off to the right was Finland and, not too far away, Russia. She was particularly proud of a peak called Kebnekaise, which she said was the highest point in Sweden, some seven thousand feet by our barbaric way of reckoning, two thousand meters by more civilized measurement.

Having already been briefed on the metric system once that day by Lou—as if I hadn't had it in college and used it in the darkroom ever since—I was getting a little tired of being educated by well-informed young ladies. I was tempted to tell this stately blonde girl that, approaching my home town of Santa Fe, New Mexico, you pass the six-thousand-foot mark several miles out of town, hit seven thousand at the Plaza—and there's nothing in the world to prevent your taking a pleasant little drive up to ten thousand in the nearby Sangre de Cristos. From there you can still keep going up a ways, if you don't mind walking. I kept my mouth shut, however. No good New Mexican wants to be heard boasting like a Texan, even in a foreign country.

At two o'clock we landed at the Kiruna airport. This seemed to consist mainly of a bleak open field and a wind sock, which was working hard. Three taxis were waiting at the fence. We all climbed in—pilots, stewardess, passengers, everybody—and were driven in to town, leaving the plane standing alone in the arctic wasteland with only the cold wind for company.

When I knocked on the door of her hotel room half an hour later, Lou called, "Come in, it isn't locked."

I stepped inside and closed the door behind me. She was sitting at the dresser in her slip, energetically brushing her short, dark, boyish hair. Her slip was a plain and practical white garment, about as sexy as a T-shirt, but her bare arms were quite nice and feminine. It occurred to me that she'd probably photograph well. That was convenient, since photogenic models might be scarce up here in the frozen north, and there are times when a human figure is almost a necessity in a picture, for scale if nothing else.

"Sit down somewhere," she said. "Let me tell you the schedule. The rest of the afternoon you're on your own. Tomorrow the company is sending a guide and a car to take us through the mine. They'll pick us up after breakfast. You'll want some views of the town, of course—maybe you can get some this afternoon—and of the railroads, particularly the one west into Norway, the spectacular one they use sending the ore over the mountains to Narvik, on the Atlantic. It's the only way of getting there except on foot; they've never managed to get a road built over those mountains. . . . But the mine's the main thing, as we agreed in Stockholm, and I've fixed it so you can get started on it tomorrow. Tomorrow night, we're going to dinner at a company bigshot's, some people named Ridderswärd. I've lied and told them we're both traveling light, so they won't expect a dinner jacket, but I hope you brought along your suit and a clean white shirt in that mountain of junk."

"Yes, ma'am," I said. "Shoes and everything." I stood behind her chair and grinned at her reflection in the mirror. "You're taking over, is that it, Lou?"

She swung around to look at me directly. Her expression was startled and innocent. "Don't be silly!" she said quickly. "I just thought. . . ." She checked herself, got up, and wrapped herself in a plain robe of blue flannel that had been lying on the bed; then she swung back to face me. "I'm terribly sorry," she said. "I didn't realize how it would look. . . . I always used to make the routine arrangements for Hal. It just . . . well, it just seemed natural to get on the phone downstairs and . . . well, I met all these people

61

the last time I was up here and. . . ."

"All right," I said. "All right, Lou. Relax."

She said, "I really didn't mean to be officious. I was just trying to help. If I bend over, will you give me a swift kick to put me in my place?"

I said, "Forget it. As a matter of fact, it sounds pretty good the way you have it arranged, except for the damn dinner, and I don't suppose we can avoid that." I laughed. "Hell, you've got yourself a job, if you want to keep at it. I've never worked with an executive assistant before, but it seems like a nice deal. I just want to warn you, there's no money in it."

She smiled. "Just shoot a good set of pictures, that's all I ask."

It was a nice scene, with all the warm sincerity of two sharpies dickering over a used car. As she turned away, in the mannish robe, I kept hearing her strange, husky voice in my head and comparing it with another voice I'd heard recently: a harsh, rasping voice that I'd assumed to be masculine, since it had come from a shadowy figure in pants. . . .

Chapter Eleven

WHEN I left her, nothing had been said about our seeing the sights together, or even meeting for dinner. Perhaps she'd been waiting for me to do the asking, but I hadn't. For one thing, coming to a new place, I always like to wander around alone, equipped with nothing but one camera and a standard lens, to get the feel of the location, before I break out the whole elaborate four-camera, nine-lens outfit and get to work. This wasn't primarily a picture-taking jaunt, of course, and my photographic disguise didn't seem to be fooling many people, but I'd been given the part and I intended to play it out. Besides, I kind of like taking pictures.

I had another reason for playing it cool where the girl was concerned. I wanted to see what would happen if I continued to maintain a pose of polite disinterest. If she was what she claimed to be, she'd presumably be relieved not to have to fight off my wolfish advances—although I don't suppose any woman really likes to be ignored. If she was something else, however, she might take certain obvious steps toward insuring my co-operation and lulling my suspicions. . . .

Despite its location ninety miles above the Arctic Circle, Kiruna turned out to be no frontier mining camp, but a solid community of brick and stone. I explored and photographed until the light began to fade and turn yellow with evening; then I had dinner in a place that served excellent food but no hard liquor, certainly no American whiskey or cocktails.

They did have beer, however, and I learned that Nordic beer comes in three grades of potency. The lowest grade is apparently a kind of beer-flavored soft drink that can safely be fed to babies; the highest is, to hear them tell it, loaded with atom juice. It sounded worth investigating, but when I asked for it I was regretfully informed that the

63

place couldn't supply it, since their license didn't extend to such violent stuff.

I had to settle for Grade Two, known as ordinary pilsener. Afterward, following directions previously given me at the hotel, I located the residence of a man named Kjellström, and rented a little black Volvo, the newest of three he had parked at the side of the house. The company might be providing a car in the morning, but I like to have transportation of my own available.

Driving away, I found myself in temporary possession of a fairly gutless little heap, far different in performance from the souped-up jobs of the same name we've been getting in the States. But it had the same nice, ugly, uncompromising lines. I understand they've gone and ruined it now, and come out with a new model looking like every other car on the road. The uninspired performance was good enough for me, under the circumstances. The gear shift didn't bother me—I keep an old pickup truck at home for back-country exploring that also has a good solid stick growing out of the floor boards—but the left-handed traffic took some getting used to, particularly with darkness coming on.

Driving slowly and cautiously, I spent half an hour locating an address on a street called Torpvägen where, according to the poop sent me by the efficient outfit in Stockholm that was arranging my hunting, I should be able to find a competent guide to take me bird-shooting. When I got there, nobody was home.

I went back to the car, turned it around, and started in the direction that seemed most likely to lead to the hotel. I was feeling pretty good, on the whole. I'd had a pleasant afternoon with my camera, and I like getting acquainted with a new type of car, and learning to drive in a new place, even a place where everybody insists on driving on the wrong side of the street. I'd relaxed; the thought of intrigue and conspiracy hadn't crossed my mind for a couple of hours. This happy feeling lasted exactly two blocks farther. Then I became aware of headlights following me. At the same time, I realized that I'd taken a wrong turn somewhere and was heading out of town.

The transition from civilization to arctic wilderness was almost instantaneous. The road turned from pavement to gravel. The last city lights died behind us. There were low, scrubby trees on both sides of the road, and I remembered the endless forests I'd seen from the plane. I stepped the accelerator down and got only a feeble response from the scant forty horsepower under the hood. Whatever was behind me had much greater reserves to call upon; it was coming up fast. At the last moment, I stood the little car on its nose, hitting the brake hard and sliding far down in the seat to give support to my head and neck in case of a rear-end collision.

There was considerable screeching and sliding from the two cars involved. I caught a glimpse of a tremendous vehicle slewing past—anyway, it looked big from where I sat in my toy Volvo. When my lights hit it, I realized it was nothing but an ordinary American Ford, the model in which somebody went taillight crazy. This was the time for me to swing my little bus around and head back for town and lights and safety, before the other guy could get his longer wheelbase reversed on that narrow road.

Being full of courage and pilsener, I climbed out and went after him instead. It wasn't quite as reckless as it sounds; in fact it was necessary. I was still, I figured, in a position where the most dangerous thing was to be smart: the dumber I looked, the safer I was. The Ford had pulled up at the side of the road ahead. Its enormous taillights cast a wicked red glow far into the trees on either hand. A man got out and came toward me, carrying something long and slender. For a moment I thought he was armed with a rifle; then I saw that it was a cane.

"Murderer!" he said. "Murderer!"

He took the cane in both hands, twisted, and pulled. There was a strange, whispering, metallic sound, and a long blade came free, slender and needle sharp, edged with red from the great, glowing lights behind him. . . .

Chapter Twelve

I HAD TIME enough—and illumination enough from the Volvo's headlights—to get a good look at him as he approached. He wasn't very big, and he had a dapper, Continental air. He was wearing a Homburg hat, required headgear for the European businessman, and his suit was dark and conservatively cut, even by local standards. There was a glint of light from a pin in his rich, glossy, flowing tie. He was wearing pearl-gray gloves. You could probably have seen your face in the mirror surface of his shoes, had the light been a little better. Having separated his sword-cane into two parts, he discarded the half he had no further use for, and come for me with the business section.

"Murderer!" he hissed. *"Förbannade mördare!"*

I wasn't with him at all, having no idea who he was or what was eating him, but a needle-pointed sword speaks a language all its own, and I ducked his first lunge and got the Solingen knife from my pocket. I flicked it open one-handed without taking my eyes from him. You grasp the blade and the weight of the handle carries it open when you snap your wrist a certain way—a show-off trick mostly, but convenient when you want to leave one hand free for attack or defense.

I had the situation figured now. His sticker was, as they often are, a three-cornered, fluted blade with no cutting edge whatever. All I had to worry about was the point. Just tease him into overreaching himself a little on the next lunge, dodge, grab the sword as he tried to recover, step inside, and use the knife, edge up, to open him up like a zipper bag from crotch to breastbone. . . .

I was a little mad, in other words. I don't like being scared, almost wrecked, and nearly skewered like a marshmallow on a toasting stick. I wasn't thinking clearly; I wasn't remembering my orders. This could be another test, like the phony beating I'd run into in Stockholm: it was fairly essential for me to remain unperforated, but I couldn't be too quick or clever at it, or too drastic. *Under no circumstances take action,* Mac had written. The instructions could be said to apply only to Caselius, but I had a hunch, if there was trouble in Washington, that any other dead bodies wouldn't be greatly appreciated. And for all I knew, this irate little fashion plate with his bodkin *was* Caselius, improbable though it might seem.

The homicidal impulse passed before any harm was done. I evaded the next lunge, all right, but my grab was deliberately clumsy, and the sword slipped through my hand. Unfortunately, the damn thing wasn't quite as dull as I'd thought. Near the point, all three edges had been honed— for better penetration, I suppose—and I got a couple of sliced fingers before I could let go.

It hurt, and I found it a little hard to remember, dodging around on the gravel with that point coming at me, just who I was supposed to be and which act I was supposed to be putting on. Well, I wasn't Matt, the innocent photographer, that was for sure. Whoever my assailant might be, he wouldn't be trying to kill me—or test me, if that was his goal—if he thought so. And I obviously wasn't Matthew, the respectable husband of Elizabeth Helm and the father of three little Helms; that part of my life was over for good, or would be as soon as the decree was final. And I wasn't Mac's boy Eric, the cold and efficient stalker of men; it wasn't time to pull that joker out of the deck, since I hadn't even identified my quarry yet, and was forbidden to act even if I had.

That left me only the character of Secret Agent Helm, the fist-fighting hero who absorbed punishment like a sponge, the defender of democracy whose attractive female associates got beat up and shot right under his nose—a slightly wised-up operative now, packing a silly little knife instead of trusting entirely to his feeble fists. Well, it was time that he showed some kind of skill with some kind of a weapon, since he wouldn't have been sent out on a job if he was completely useless. I wasn't very fond of this guy, he was pretty much a moron, but I did have a certain interest in keeping him alive.

"*Mördare!*" the little man panted. "Dirty killer. Pig!" If it was an act, he was putting his heart into it. He was

67

getting warmed up now, and he'd fenced in his time, but edged and pointed tools have always been my specialty. Ever since I was a kid with a wooden sword and a shield made out of Dad's old tobacco cans, I've had a fondness for the shining blades. A gun, after all, is good for nothing but killing. With a knife, as the oldtimers used to say, when you've nothing more interesting to do, you can always whittle.

I wiped my cut left hand on my pants, and switched the knife over, in time to knock aside his sword as it came at me again. At the same instant I ducked and picked up the weapon he'd discarded, perhaps thinking it no weapon at all, perhaps wanting to see if I had sense enough and skill enough to use it. But I had no choice; I couldn't keep him off forever with less than four inches of steel. I scooped it up: about thirty inches of strong and slender cane, tipped with a nice brass ferrule. Now I had the cane in my right hand and the knife in my left. It was the old Italian sword-and-dagger routine. They could also do mean things with a cloak, blinding an opponent or entangling his blade, but I didn't have a cloak handy.

"All right, Buster," I panted. "I don't know what's got you so burned up, but if you want to fence, let's fence! I used to be pretty good at this in college."

He came in again fast, and I took his blade on the cane, deflected it neatly, and lunged in my turn, driving the shiny brass ferrule straight at his eyes. He saved himself only by a frantic last-minute parry. It had been a long time, and I no longer remembered quarte from tierce, but my wrist hadn't forgotten nearly as much as my mind.

His part of the sword-cane was somewhat longer than mine, and sharper, but I also had the knife, and obviously he'd never played that game before. It's not considered respectable in contemporary *salles des armes*. I had the reach on him by several inches, enough to compensate for the difference in weapons, and the brass-tipped cane was plenty sharp enough to destroy a man's eye or throat.

It was a weird scene, I suppose, on that deserted road up near the frozen top of the world, but I was too busy to appreciate it fully. We'd dance from the dull red glow of the Ford's taillights into the bright white glare of the headlights of the Volvo, each trying to keep the more intense illumination in the other's eyes.

We got better as we went along. The little man had a strong wrist and he was fast on his feet; he'd obviously been a good épée-and-foil man in his day, although like me he was rusty now. Sword against sword he might well have taken me. But he was fighting the handicap of the knife and his own anger, real or pretended. Time and again the short Solingen blade would break up a classic attack pattern that had never been designed for use against a two-weapon defense. And time and again he'd drive in furiously when he should have taken it easy and figured me out. He kept trying for the heart when he should have gone for an exposed wrist or arm.

His tie was flapping loose now; his hat was gone and his shoes were dusty. His face was shiny and sweating; so was mine, no doubt. He came in again, and as I parried I realized that he was tiring: his point was far out of line. There's an old trick whereby you can, theoretically, disarm a man if he'll stand still for it. I don't suppose it was ever used in actual combat, any more than any of the old Western gunmen ever used such fancy stunts as the highwayman's roll or the border shift. You don't generally do juggling tricks when your life's at stake.

But still, it was a theoretical possibility, and he was right in position for it, and I had to do something with him that wasn't lethal. I made a sharp counter-clockwise circle with the cane—I've forgotten the technical name of the maneuver—catching that wide point and spinning it around, twisting the weapon in his grasp. . . .

An alert swordsman, in good condition, would simply have come smoothly around my blade, or cane, and continued his attack; but the little man's reflexes were slowing, his wrist was tired, and the sudden wrench caught him by surprise, took the sword away from him, and sent it flying across the road. He stood there for a moment, disarmed and vulnerable, and I couldn't decide what the hell to do with him. I guess I was a bit tired, too.

When I moved, it was too late. He gave a kind of sob and ran after his weapon. He beat me to it and picked it up and came at me again, but he wasn't fencing any more. He had the sword in both hands and he was wielding it like a club, beating at my head and shoulders. He was crying with frustration and anger as he whacked away, trying to chop me down like a tree.

It was all I could do to defend myself against the crazy attack. I could kill him, all right—he was wide open, with his arms above his head like that, and one straight-armed lunge would have driven the brass-tipped cane through the cartilages of his throat—but I wasn't supposed to kill anybody. *Under no circumstances. This is an order. This is an order.* Suddenly I had too many weapons. My hands were full; I had to get rid of something if I was going to take him alive, although this seemed to have most of the pleasant aspects of getting a living, spitting bobcat out of a tree.

I parried a two-handed cut with the sword that would have laid my scalp open even if the weapon didn't have a real edge on it. I threw my arms about the little man, dropped everything and, clutching him desperately—if he got free now, he could run me through in an instant—I gave him the knee just as hard and dirty as I could. When he doubled up, I clubbed him on the back of the head, not with the edge of the hand to break his neck, but just with the heel of my fist, like a hammer, to drive him down into the road. He went down, and curled up like a baby, hugging himself where it hurt.

Breathing hard, I retrieved my knife. I picked up the sword, and the cane sheath, and fitted them back together. It was a beautiful job of workmanship: you couldn't see the joint at all. I picked up the Homburg hat and dusted it off, and carried it back to the little guy, who was still lying there. My left hand ached, and I didn't feel a bit sorry for him, although I had to admit, in all honesty, that he'd put on a damn good show. Whether it was genuine or phony remained to be determined. I bent over to hear what he was moaning. I caught a name, and leaned closer.

"Sara," he was whimpering. "I did my best, Sara. I am sorry." Then he looked up at me. "I am ready," he said more clearly. "If I were just a little bigger. . . . But I am ready now. Kill me, murderer, as you did her!"

Chapter Thirteen

IT TOOK us a while to get things straightened out. When he'd finally become reconciled to not dying heroically at my hands, the little man told me he was Sara Lundgren's fiancé, Raoul Carlsson, of the house of Carlsson and LeClaire, women's clothing, Stockholm, Paris, London, Rome. He'd met Sara at her dress shop in the line of business, it seemed, and romance had flowered.

He'd been worried about his Sara lately, however. She'd seemed preoccupied and unhappy, he said. Finally, when she stood him up for lunch and then called up later the same day from a certain hotel to cancel their dinner engagement for reasons that didn't ring quite true, he'd taken it upon himself to go there and . . . well, to tell the truth, he'd spied on her. For her own good, of course, not because he was the least bit jealous. He merely wanted to know what was troubling her so that he could help.

Watching her surreptitiously as she waited in the hotel lobby, he'd soon realized that she, in turn, was busy watching for somebody else. He'd seen me come through the lobby with Lou Taylor. Sara had followed us, and he'd followed Sara. After dinner, he'd trailed us all back to the hotel. Then Sara had got her car and driven into the park. He'd been behind her until she stopped. She got away from him briefly while he was looking for a suitable place to leave his own car. When he got back to the parking lot on foot, her fancy Volkswagen was standing there empty.

He'd waited in the bushes for her to return. He'd seen her come back to the car with me. We'd had a long conversation, not as friendly as it might have been, he thought. I'd left abruptly, he thought in anger, and disappeared into the darkness. Almost immediately, as if dispatched by me, two men had come and dragged Sara out of her car and carried her off in the direction I'd taken. While he, Carlsson, was

71

still trying to make his way after her through the trees and darkness, there had been shots. He'd come to the edge of the clearing and seen me standing there, looking grim and terrible. At my feet was his beloved, his Sara, lying on the ground, brutally beaten and shot to death. He'd started forward, but the police had come. . . .

"Why didn't you tell them about me?" I asked, when he stopped.

He shrugged his shoulders expressively. "They would have put you in prison where I could not reach you. I was crazy with grief and anger. I was going to punish you myself, not give you to some stupid policeman!" After a moment, he went on: "I slipped away. I learned your name at the hotel. When you left, in the morning, it was easy to determine your destination. I followed."

"With your little sword-cane," I said dryly.

He shrugged again. "Pistols are not so common here as they are in your country, Herr Helm. It was the only weapon I owned. I thought it would suffice. I did not expect to meet a swordsman with an American passport." He grimaced. "You are skillful, sir, but that little knife, I do not think that was quite fair." After a moment, he said, "You cannot tell me this secret business in which, you say, my Sara was engaged, that led to her death? You cannot tell me who killed her?"

I said, "No, but I can assure you the man will be taken care of."

That was big talk, for someone whose hands were tied by official orders, but I had to say something to get this little firebrand out of my hair. The situation was complex enough without being loused up further by vengeful amateurs. I finally got him to promise to go back to Stockholm and leave everything to me. I took his home address and telephone number, and promised to notify him when I had something to notify him about. I watched him get into his big American car and drive away. Then I got into my little Volvo, drove back to the hotel, stuck some bandaids on my fingers, and went to bed.

In the morning, I had my breakfast in a corner of the hotel dining room, which I shared, for the moment, only with a pair of railroad workers and a tourist couple from Norway—the language sounds like badly garbled Swedish, to a Swede. Outside the windows, it was a bright, clear fall day. I hoped it would stay that way, for photography's sake. I sipped my coffee, and nibbled at the stuff on my plate, and thought about Mr. Raoul Carlsson, which was a waste of time. If the little man was kidding me, I'd know more about it when Vance made his report, I hoped within the next day or two.

A shadow fell across the table. "Are you thinking deep thoughts?" Lou Taylor asked. "If so, I'll go away."

I rose and helped her with her chair. She was wearing the same rust-brown skirt and sweater as yesterday, with the same sturdy walking shoes. She had a trench coat with her, but she'd dropped it on a chair. As far as I'm concerned, a trench coat looks fine on Alan Ladd, and not bad on Marlene Dietrich, but she wasn't either one.

She smiled at me across the table, and stopped smiling abruptly. "What happened to your hand?"

I glanced at my bandaged fingers. "I cut it," I said. "I dropped a glass and cut myself picking up the pieces."

She said dryly, "I think you'd better get yourself another girl, Matt."

I frowned. "What does that mean? Are you bowing out?"

"Oh, I wasn't referring to myself," she said, laughing quickly. "I mean, your night girl, the one who plays so rough. A black eye yesterday, two cut fingers today—or did she bite you in an excess of passion?"

"Keep it clean, now."

"Well, what do you do nights, to get yourself all beat up like that, if it isn't a girl? The secret life of Matthew Helm. . . . Helm?" she said. "Is that a Swedish name?"

"More or less," I said. "It used to be fancier, but Dad whittled it down to something even Yankees could pronounce."

"I thought you must have some Scandinavian blood, or you wouldn't be sitting there eating that stuff so calmly. Fish for breakfast, my God!" She glanced at her watch. "Well, we'd better hurry; they'll be here in ten minutes. Do you think I could possibly promote a simple cup of black coffee and some toast? *Rostat bröd*, they call it," she said. "That means, literally, roasted bread. . . ."

It was hard to figure her. If she was on the other team, she was very good indeed. She'd have been told I knew Swedish perfectly well, yet here she was calmly instructing me in the language of my ancestors, as she'd taught me

73

their system of measurement the day before. Well, it was always nice to deal with people who knew their business.

When the company car arrived, right on schedule, it turned out to be a long, black, dignified-looking old Chrysler limousine complete with one middle-aged gent in a chauffeur's cap to drive it, and one young guy named Lindström to answer our questions and keep us out of trouble. The two men helped me load my paraphernalia aboard; then we drove to the mine entrance, less than a mile from the hotel, and were passed through the gate with some formality. We took a road up the side of a mountain named Kirnnavaara—*vaara* means mountain in Finnish, Lou informed me. A great many of the local place names show the Finnish influence, she said, since the border is less than a hundred miles away.

It wasn't quite Pike's Peak, but it was a respectable hill nevertheless. Near the top, as high as the road went, we stopped and got out at a wide place, like one of the scenic-view parking areas you find along mountain roads back home. There was a cold wind up here, and the view was worth looking at in both directions. Outwards, to the east, we could see the arctic wilderness in gaudy autumn colors running clear to the horizon without much sign of civilization except for the town practically at our feet. Inwards, to the west, we were looking straight down a man-made canyon cut through the heart of the mountain itself.

They'd taken a slice right out of the middle of it, like a dentist preparing a tooth for a gold inlay; and the funny thing was, the place looked familiar. I knew a dozen canyons like it back home: the color and shape were just right. Except for the shacks and machines far down at the bottom, I could have been looking into a section of the canyon of the San Juan, or the Salt River, or even certain parts of the Rio Grande. It was quite a sight, when you considered that it had practically been dug by hand.

I got to work, to the accompaniment of a running lecture by Lindström on the technical aspects of the operation, most of which I already knew from reading Lou's article. We photographed the ten-o'clock blast: they fire off about two hundred kilograms of dynamite morning and evening to knock the stuff loose so the power shovels can handle it. Two hundred kilograms, Lou informed me, is better than four hundred pounds. It made as much noise as you'd expect, and there was a satisfactory amount of dust and flying debris for the camera. After the fumes had cleared, we went below and spent the day taking pictures of tunnels and tracks and buildings and machines and magnetite ore in all shapes and manifestations.

Twice we were stopped by officious persons who came up to tell us that picture-taking was *förbjuden* in these sacred precincts, but Lou had arranged for the proper *tillstånd*, or permission, so the guardians of security were forced to retire in confusion. I had to hand it to the girl. She had the situation completely under control. She also knew exactly what she wanted, and she wasn't a bit bashful about telling me what it was. All I had to do was aim the box as ordered and push the button. It wasn't the way I was accustomed to working, but I let it go, contenting myself with taking an extra shot here and there when it looked as if she was passing up something nice and picturesque.

It was a hard day, and I was glad I was in reasonable condition; she didn't drag her feet much. In the evening, aside from a little dust here and there, and a run in one stocking due to an unfortunate encounter with some machinery—for which Herr Lindström had apologized profusely—she looked as fresh as a peach on the tree.

"Well, we made a good start today," she said cheerfully, helping me gather up the equipment as the limousine drove away. "Another day should see us finished there, if the weather holds. Then one more day to cover some of the smaller mines in the area, and after that we'll start working our way back down along the railroad toward Luleå. There's a place called Stora Malmberget, which means The Great Ore Mountain—isn't that a wonderful name?—and then I want the docks at Luleå, of course. All the ore goes out that way in summer, and down through the Baltic by ship, but after the ice comes in the fall they have to send it over the mountains to Narvik, which stays open all year because of the Gulf Stream. We'll come back here and finish up the job with that end of the operation. I certainly hope the weather stays clear. It was fine today, wasn't it?"

She sounded enthusiastic and full of energy, as if she'd just got out of bed. She sounded as if this article really meant something to her. She was a hard kid to figure out.

"Yes," I said, "it was fine." We were outside my door

now. I opened up and shoved the stuff I was carrying inside, and relieved her of her burdens. "Well, thanks for the helping hand. How about a drink?"

She shook her head. "No, thanks, and if you don't mind a little advice, you'd better not have one, either. We're due out for dinner in—" she glanced at her watch—"in twenty minutes, and unless you know your capacity and Swedish dinners better than I think you do, you won't want to get a head start. They won't serve us much in the way of cocktails, but that's about the only alcoholic beverage they'll skimp on in any way. So brace yourself, man, brace yourself."

"Yes, ma'am," I said meekly, and went in to clean myself up for the ordeal.

Chapter Fourteen

THE HOUSE was a large one, and looked pleasantly old-fashioned—two stories and a big attic, at a guess; no ranch houses or split levels here, thank you. We shook hands with the host and hostess, with a small son and daughter who bowed and curtsied prettily, and with a visiting fireman with the title of *Direktör*, a title that was shared by our host, a lean man in his forties. In Sweden, I was catching on, everybody has a title, and if your name is Jones and you're in charge of the city pound, you'll be introduced everywhere as Chief Dogcatcher Jones. Women are, on the whole, exempt from this formality, so Lou remained Mrs. Taylor, but I became Journalist Helm.

"There is someone here who wishes much to meet you," said our hostess, a slender, gray-haired woman who had a little trouble with her English. "A guest from Stockholm. She was much interested when she heard we were entertaining a gentleman named Helm from America. She thinks you may be distantly related. Ah, here she comes now."

I looked around and saw a girl in a shiny blue dress coming down the stairs. My first impression was that she must have borrowed the dress from a very rich old maiden aunt. It had that look of magnificent quality and complete lack of style and suitability. . . . As I say, the first thing I noticed was the frumpy, shiny dress. Then I saw that the kid was beautiful.

It's not a word I use lightly. It hasn't got anything to do with big bosoms and sexy rear ends, in my interpretation, nor even with pretty faces. Hollywood, for instance, is full of women you can bear to look at and wouldn't mind going to bed with. They even photograph fairly well. But they're not beautiful, and the very few who are spoil it by working too hard at it.

This girl wasn't working at all. She didn't do anything

77

as she came down the stairs, she just came down the damn stairs. She hadn't put anything on her face you could notice except some lipstick, and that was the wrong color—that ghastly pale morgue-pink stuff—and it didn't make a damn bit of difference. She was beautiful, and that was all there was to it. It made you want to cry for all the women in the world who were striving so hard for it and would never achieve it.

She was in her early twenties, rather tall and by no means fragile: she had a nice, durable, well-put-together look. She wasn't even the kind of spectacular blonde you often get in that country. She had straight, light-brown hair that she didn't, apparently, pay much attention to except to brush it hard morning and night. It was long enough to reach her shoulders. She had blue eyes. What difference does it make? You can't add it up or analyze it. It's just there. I will admit that I might be slightly prejudiced. I'm a sucker for that heartbreaking young-and-innocent look, particularly in combination with a fair complexion, after all the years I've spent in a land of dark and sultry Spanish-American beauties who knew everything before they were born.

I had a chance to watch her a little longer as she was first introduced to Lou, three or four years older, and then had the visiting Director, a pompous middle-aged man—I never did learn what he was Director of—introduced to her. Then it was my turn.

"Elin, this is Journalist Helm, from America," our hostess said. "Herr Helm, Fröken von Hoffman." *Fröken*, as Lou would have hastened to explain, merely means "Miss" in Swedish.

The girl held out her hand. "Yes," she said, "I have been hoping to meet you, Herr Helm, since I learned in Stockholm you were in this country. We are related, you know. Very, very distant cousins, I think."

My parents had often talked about coming back here to visit relatives. I did have some, somewhere. This girl could be one. I wasn't going to disown her, that was for sure.

"I didn't know," I said, "but I certainly won't argue the point, Cousin Ellen."

"Elin," she said, smiling. "*Ay*-linn. I always have that difficulty with Englishmen and Americans. They always want to christen me Ellen or Elaine, but it really is Elin."

Then some more people came in, and she was borne away

on a new tide of introductions and handshaking. There was none of the pre-food dawdling here that you get at home. Everybody being present at the appointed hour, our hostess barely gave us time to absorb the cocktails, so-called, that had been put into our hands—I think they were supposed to be Manhattans, God help them—then the dining-room doors were thrown open and we were introduced to the main business of the evening. It seemed on the whole like an improvement over spending two hours getting blotto while waiting for latecomers to make dramatic, breathless entrances with phony excuses.

Any previous liquor shortage was more than made up during the meal, as Lou had warned me it would be. There were beer and two different kinds of wine, and a promise of cognac to come. The table settings were awe-inspiring to a simple New Mexico boy, and for a while I was kept busy noticing who was eating what with what. It was quite a layout to have to tackle without a manual of instructions. My conversation therefore consisted of letting my hostess explain to me the Swedish art of toast-drinking: you look firmly into the eyes of the person you wish to honor, both parties drink, and then you look again before putting your glass down.

You're not, it seems, supposed to *skål* your host and hostess, and you're supposed to wait for an older or more important man to take the initiative, after which you must soon return the courtesy, but any lady at the table except your hostess is fair game. In the old days, I was told, a lady could not propose a *skål*—it would have been considered very forward of her—nor was it considered proper for her to drink without a social excuse, so an unpopular girl could perish of thirst with a full glass of wine in front of her.

Having learned all this, I put it to use. I picked up my glass and saluted the kid on the other side of me.

"*Skål*, Cousin Elin," I said.

She looked me in the eyes, as custom demanded, and smiled. "*Skål*, Cousin . . . Matthew? That is the same as our Matthias, is it not? Do you speak any Swedish at all?"

I shook my head. "I knew a few words when I was a boy, but I've forgotten most of them."

"That is too bad," she said. "I speak English very badly."

"Uhuh," I said. "Half the population of America should

79

speak it as badly as you do. How did you happen to hear of me in Stockholm?"

She said, "It is very simple. You like to hunt, do you not? A man in Stockholm whose business is arranging hunts for foreigners called up old *Överste* Stjernhjelm at Torsåter—*Överste* means Colonel, you know. There is an *Älg*-hunt at Torsäter in a week or two. Torsäter is the family estate near Uppsala, one of our two big University towns, sixty kilometers north of Stockholm, about forty of your English miles. *Älg*, that is our Swedish moose, not as big as your Canadian variety—"

She wasn't getting very far. I said, "Cousin, why don't you just tell the story? When you throw me a word I don't know, I'll stop you."

She laughed. "All right, but you said you didn't know Swedish. . . . There are usually not many strangers at the Torsäter hunt. It is a small neighborhood affair, but the man in Stockholm said he had an American client, a sportsman and journalist who wanted to write about some typical Swedish hunting, and it would be very nice if Colonel Stjernhjelm would invite him to be a guest. The colonel was not really interested, until he heard that your name was Helm. He remembered that a cousin of his had emigrated to America many years ago and shortened his name. He remembered that there had been a son. The colonel, like many of our old retired people, is very interested in genealogy. Having made certain from his records that you were a member of the family, he tried to reach you in Stockholm, but you had already left. He knew I was planning a visit here, so he called me and asked me to get in touch with you."

I grinned. "Just get in touch?"

She said, with some embarrassment, "Well, he did want me to let him know what kind of a person you were. So you must behave yourself while I have you under observation, Cousin Matthias, so I can write a favorable report to the colonel. Then he will invite you hunting, I am sure."

I said, "All right, I'll be good. Now tell me how we got to be cousins."

"Very, very distant cousins," she said, smiling. "It is rather complicated, but I think it was this way: back in 1652, two brothers von Hoffman came here from Germany. One of them married a Miss Stjernhjelm, whose brother was a direct ancestor of yours. The other married another nice Swedish girl and became an ancestor of mine. I hope this is quite clear. If it is not, I'm sure Colonel Stjern-hjelm will be delighted to explain it to you when you return south. He has all kinds of genealogical tables at Torsäter."

I glanced at her. "Sixteen fifty-two, you say?"

She smiled again. "Yes. As I told you, it is not a very close relationship."

Then, for some reason, she blushed a little. I hadn't seen a girl do that in years.

Chapter Fifteen

WHEN it was time to leave, our host was shocked to learn that Lou and I had arrived in a car and now intended to drive back to the hotel. It seems that the Swedish laws against drunken driving are so strict that you don't ever drive to a party unless one occupant of the car intends not to drink at all. Otherwise you play safe and take a cab. We were, of course, quite sober and capable, our host agreed, but we'd both inbibed detectable quantities of alcohol, and we couldn't be allowed to run the risk. A taxi would take us to the hotel, and somebody would deliver our car there in the morning.

At the hotel, we climbed the stairs in silence, and stopped at Lou's door.

"I won't ask you in for a drink," she said. "It would be a crime to dump whisky on top of all that lovely wine and cognac. Besides, I don't think I could stay awake. Good night, Matt."

"Good night," I said, and crossed the hall to my own room, let myself in, closed the door behind me, and grinned wryly. Apparently she'd decided to give me some of my own medicine: two could play it cool as well as one. I yawned, undressed, and went to bed.

Sleep washed over me in a wave, but just as I was losing my last contact with reality, I heard a sound that made me wide awake again. Somewhere an ancient hinge had creaked softly. I listened intently and heard the click of a high heel in the hall; Lou was leaving her room. Well, she could be paying a visit to the communal plumbing. Her room, like mine, boasted only a small curtained cubicle with a lavatory and a neat little locker containing a white enamel receptacle for emergency use.

I waited, but she didn't return. I didn't even consider trying to follow her. It was a complicated game we were playing, but I still thought the guy who would win was the guy who could act dumbest. To hell with her and her midnight expeditions. It was something I knew that she didn't know I knew. It was a point for our side. Well, call it half a point. I turned over in bed and closed my eyes.

Nothing happened. Suddenly I had the keyed-up feeling you get from a lot of liquor partially neutralized by a lot of coffee. Sleep was no longer anywhere around. I stood it as long as I could; then I got up and walked around the bed to the window and looked out. The window was a casement type without screens, standard in this country. There was something strange and a little shocking about standing at a second-floor window completely exposed to the great outdoors. You get so used to looking at the world through wire netting that you feel naked and unsafe when it's taken away.

Although it was midnight, the sky was still lighter than it would have been in Santa Fe, New Mexico: we have black night skies at home, with brilliant stars. This wasn't much of a display, by comparison. My window faced a lake. I'd forgotten the name, but it would end in -järvi, since järvi was the Finnish word for lake and, as Lou had pointed out, the Finnish influence was strong here, within a hundred miles of the border. Standing there, I could feel geography crowding me—a feeling you never get at home. But here I was standing in a wedge of one little country, Sweden, thrust up between two others, Norway and Finland. And behind Finland was Russia and the arctic port of Murmansk. . . .

A movement in the bushes drew my attention, and Lou Taylor came into sight some distance away. She'd left her coat in her room, apparently. With her dark hair, in her black dress, she was almost invisible. By the time I saw her, it was too late for me to duck out of sight. She was already looking up toward my window, where my face would be shining like a neon sign against the blackness of the room behind me. She turned quickly to warn the person with her, but he didn't catch the signal in time. As he straightened up, after ducking a branch, I recognized the big, football-player shape of the man I'd met in her Stockholm hotel room: Jim Wellington.

I stood there watching them. Having already been seen, they took time to finish whatever they'd been talking about.

83

She asked a question. Whatever she wanted, he wasn't giving it. He turned and disappeared into the bushes. She made her way into the clear, with due regard for her dress and nylons and fragile shoes. She vanished around the corner of the hotel without looking up at me again.

It was getting cold in the room. I closed the window and drew the shade. The bed didn't attract me any more strongly than before. I found my dressing gown, put it on, and turned on the light. I stood for a moment looking at the films from the day's shooting lined up on the bureau: five rolls of color and three of black-and-white. This didn't actually mean that I'd taken more subjects in Kodachrome; on the contrary, I'd taken less, but color is trickier than black-and-white and therefore I habitually protect each color exposure by bracketing it with two others, one longer and one shorter. It's cheaper in the long run than going back for retakes.

It was a poor harvest for a whole day's work, showing that my heart had not been in it. On a job that appeals to me, I can burn up several times that amount of film in a day and never work up a sweat. But circumstances hadn't been conducive to a fine, free, frenzy of inspiration. I'd been practically told what to shoot; I'd had little incentive to branch out on my own.

The knock on the door didn't make me jump very high. I'd already heard her footsteps in the hall. I walked over and let her in. When I turned, after closing the door behind her, she was taking advantage of the light to examine her stockings for runs and her dress for dust and woods debris. It was the same smoothly fitting jersey dress she'd worn to dinner in Stockholm, with the big bunch of satin at the hip.

"I thought you were asleep." Her voice was flat.

"I was heading that way, but you woke me up by going out," I said. "What's that Wellington character doing up here in Kiruna, anyway?"

She stalled briefly. "So you recognized him?"

I said, "A man that size is hard to miss."

It occurred to me suddenly that of all the people involved to date, Jim Wellington was the only one big enough to stick on a phony beard and give a rumbling laugh and bear a reasonable resemblance to Hal Taylor's description of Caselius.

Lou Taylor had turned away from me. She reached out absently and rearranged the films on the dresser before speaking. "What if I were to tell you it's none of your damn business what he's doing here?" she said at last.

I said, "I might not agree with you. But there wouldn't be much I could do about it, would there?"

She glanced at me over her shoulder. After a moment, she reached out and picked up one of the film cartridges. "Are all these from today? I didn't know we'd taken so many."

"That's not many," I said. "You should see me go through the stuff when I really get warmed up."

"What will you do with them now? Are you going to develop them right away?"

"No," I said. "The color has to go to a lab in Stockholm, anyway. I can't do that myself. The black-and-white I'll save until I have a place with reasonable facilities to work in. Maybe I can scare up somebody in Stockholm with a real darkroom I can use. I hate working out of a hotel closet." After a moment, I asked, "Do you owe this Wellington character anything?"

She put the film down and turned slowly to face me. Everything was sharp and clear. We were two people who'd been around. I'd caught her out, and I could now waste a lot of time asking a bunch of silly questions and forcing her to think up a bunch of equally silly answers. The end would be the same. We'd wind up facing each other like this, neither knowing any more about the other than before. There was really only one thing we needed to know, and only one way of finding it out.

"Why, no," she said slowly, "I wouldn't say I owe Jim Wellington a thing." Then, still watching me carefully, she said, "You've been pretending not to like me much, haven't you?"

"Yes," I said. "That's right. Pretending. I had some thought of keeping this strictly business."

"That," she said, coming forward, "was a very silly idea, wasn't it?"

Chapter Sixteen

THIS WAS the land of the Midnight Sun, and while it was past the season for that particular display— it happens only around midsummer—the evenings were still late and the mornings were still early. Presently the long winter night would descend over the land, but not quite yet. It seemed very soon that there was light at the window.

She said, "I'd better get back to my room, darling."

"No hurry," I said. "It's early, and the Swedes are a tolerant people, anyway."

She said, "I was awfully lonely, darling." After a while she said, "Matt?"

"Yes?"

"How do you think we ought to run this?"

I thought that over for a moment. "You mean, like strictly for laughs?"

"Yes. Like that, or like some other way. How do you want it?"

"I don't know," I said. "It'll take some thought. I haven't had too much experience along these lines."

"I'm glad. I haven't, either." After a little, she said, "I suppose we could act cool and sophisticated about the whole thing."

"That's it," I said. "That's me. Cool. Sophisticated."

"Matt."

"Yes."

"It's a lousy business, isn't it?"

She shouldn't have said that. It admitted everything, about both of us. It gave everything away, and we'd been doing fine. It had been a smooth, polished act on both sides, one move leading to the next without a stumble or a missed cue; and then, like a sentimental amateur, she went and deliberately tossed the whole slick routine overboard. Suddenly we weren't actors any longer. We weren't dedicated agents, either, robots operating expertly in that kind of unreal borderland that exists on the edge of violence. We were just two real people without any clothes on lying in the same bed.

I raised my head to look at her. Her face was a pale shape against the whiter pillow. Her dark hair was no longer brushed smoothly back over her small, exposed ears. It was kind of tousled now, and she looked cute that way. She was really a hell of a nice-looking girl, in a slim and economical sort of way. Her bare shoulders looked very naked in the cold room. I pulled up the blanket and tucked it around her.

"Yes," I said, "but we don't have to make it any lousier than necessary."

She said, "Don't trust me, Matt. And don't ask me any questions."

"You took the words right out of my mouth."

"All right," she said. "As long as we both understand."

I said, "You're green, kid. You're real smart, but you're an amateur, aren't you? A pro wouldn't have given it all away like you just did. She'd have left me guessing."

She said, "You gave yourself away, too."

"Sure," I said, "but you knew about me. You've known about me all along. I still wasn't quite sure about you."

"Well, now you know," she said, "something. But are you sure what?" she laughed softly. "I really have to go. Where's my dress?"

"I don't know," I said, "but there seems to be somebody's brassiere hanging on the foot of the bed."

"The hell with my brassiere," she said. "I'm not going to a formal reception, just across the hall."

I lay and watched her get up and turn on the light. She found her dress on a chair, shook it out, examined it, pulled it on, fastened it up, and stepped into her shoes. She went to the dresser, looked at herself in the mirror, and pushed helplessly at her hair. She gave that up, and came back to the bed to gather up the rest of her clothes.

"Matt."

"Yes?"

"I'll double-cross you without blinking an eye, darling. You know that, don't you?"

"Don't talk so tough," I said lazily. "You'll scare me. Reach in my right pants pocket."

87

She glanced at me, picked up my pants, and did as I'd asked. She fumbled around among some change and came out with the knife. I sat up, took it from her, and did the flick-it-open trick. Her eyes widened slightly at sight of the sharp, slender blade.

"Meet Baby," I said. "Don't kid yourself, Lou. If you know anything about me at all, you know what I'm here for. It's in the open now, that's all. This doesn't change anything. Don't get in my way. I'd hate to have to hurt you."

We'd had a moment of honesty, but it was slipping away from us fast. We were starting to hedge on our bets. We were falling enthusiastically into our new roles as star-crossed lovers, a jet-age Romeo and Juliet, on opposite sides of the fence. Too much frankness can be as much a lie as too little. Her speech about double-crossing had been unnecessary; she'd already warned me not to trust her. If you say "Don't trust me, darling" often enough, you can make the warning lose its effect.

As for me, I was brandishing a knife and making blood-curdling speeches: good old bone-headed, fist-fighting Secret Agent Helm flexing his muscles before a lady he'd just laid.

I think we both felt a kind of sadness as we looked at each other, knowing we were losing something we might never find again. I closed the knife abruptly and tossed it on top of my pants on the chair.

She said, "Well, I'll see you at breakfast, Matt," and leaned over to kiss me, and I put my arm about her just above the knees, holding her by the bed. "No, let me go, darling," she said. "It's getting late."

"Yes," I said. "Have you seen yourself like that?"

She frowned. "You mean my hair? I know it's a mess, but whose fault—"

"No, I don't mean your hair," I said, and she looked down at herself quickly, where I was looking, and seemed a little startled to see the way her unconfined breasts made themselves quite obvious through the clinging wool jersey of her dress. It was the same elsewhere. It was really quite a thing: the simple, discreet black dress with its party touch of satin at the waist and so obviously nothing but Lou inside it. She'd have been much more respectable in a transparent negligee.

She murmured, rather abashed, "I didn't realize. . . . I look practically indecent, don't I?"

"Practically?"

She laughed, and shaped the black cloth to her breasts with her hands, a little defiantly. "They're kind of small," she said. "I always wondered if any other animal besides man . . . I mean, do you think bulls, for instance, go for the cows with the biggest udders?"

"Don't be snide," I said. "You're just jealous."

"Naturally," she said. "I'd just love to have them out to here . . . well, I guess I wouldn't, really. Think of the responsibility. It would be like owning a couple of priceless works of art. This way, I don't have to spend my life living up to them."

I said, "If current fashions continue, I suppose we'll eventually wind up with a whole race of skinny women with giant tits."

She said, quite primly, "I think the discussion has gone far enough in that direction."

She was a funny girl. "Do you object to the word?" I asked.

"Yes," she said, and tried to free herself again. "And I don't really want to go to bed with you again right now, certainly not with my one good dress on, so please let me . . . *Matt!*"

I'd pulled her down on top of me. "You should have thought of that—" I said, rather breathlessly, as, holding her in my arms, I reversed our positions by rolling over with her—"you should have thought of that before you started looking so goddamn sexy."

"Matt!" she wailed, struggling ineffectually among the bedclothes. "Matt, I really don't want. . . . Oh, all right darling," she breathed, "all right, all right, just give me a chance to kick my shoes off, will you, and please be careful of my dress!"

Chapter Seventeen

LATER, alone in the room, I shaved and dressed and organized my equipment for the day's shooting. I mean, it would have been nicer to spend a few lazy hours thinking about nothing but love, but it just wasn't practical. As I was going out the door, I glanced back to see if I'd forgotten anything. Yesterday's films, still lined up on the dresser, caught my eye.

I regarded them for a moment, a little grimly. Then I set my gear down, closed the door, and went over there. What I was thinking now seemed terribly suspicious and disloyal. She was a nice kid and she'd been as sweet as she could be—but she'd also displayed some curiosity last night, maybe casual, maybe not, about just how and where I planned to get the stuff processed and printed.

Much as I hated to spoil what had happened between us with cynical afterthoughts, I couldn't help remembering that I'd been playing it cool deliberately to see just what she'd do in the way of insuring my co-operation and lulling my suspicions. Well, she'd gone and done it, there was no denying that. Maybe she'd done it because she liked me, but one thing you learn very quickly in this business is not to take for granted that you're just naturally irresistible to lonely women. Whatever her reasons, whatever her motives, she'd certainly allowed the businesslike relationship between us to be changed into something considerably more intimate.

I couldn't afford to ignore the warning, or her display of curiosity about the films. It might mean nothing, of course, but I had to consider the possibility, at least, that these pix and the others I'd be taking in her company might have more significance than appeared on the surface. A few simple precautions seemed in order.

I sighed for my lost faith and innocence, went to the closet, and got out one of the metal .50-caliber cartridge boxes I use for preserving my main film supply. I dug out five unexposed rolls of Kodachrome and three unexposed rolls of black-and-white, still in the factory cartons. I sat down on the bed and opened the virgin film cartons carefully, breaking loose the adhesive with my knife without tearing the cardboard flaps.

Then I removed the unexposed films inside and carefully substituted the exposed films from the dresser. I glued the cartons shut again with patent stickum from my repair kit, and made a tiny identifying mark on each of the doctored cartons—a dot in the loop of the "a" in Kodak, if you must know—and buried all eight of them at the bottom of the box of fresh film, hoping I wouldn't grab one by mistake some day when I was in a hurry.

I turned to the new films, and drew each five-foot film strip completely out of its metal cartridge, exposing it to light so that, if developed, it would turn totally black. No one would ever be able to determine whether or not it had ever held a real photographic image. There's nothing as permanent and irrevocable as fogging a film, except killing a man.

I rolled all the films back into the cartridges by hand, got an empty camera, and one by one loaded them into the instrument, wound them a little way, and rewound them again. This gave the proper reverse curl to the leaders, as if they'd actually been used. I was getting pretty tricky now, but there's no sense pulling a gag like that unless you make it good. I marked each fogged roll with an authentic-looking number to correspond with the data in my notebook. Finally I put the film cartridges in a neat row on the dresser, where they looked exactly like the films that had stood there before.

Probably I was just wasting my time. However, I had plenty of film to spare, and if I was wrong there was little harm done. It seemed about time to start taking a few obvious precautions, anyway. I had to remember that the opposition had tested me carefully at least once and maybe twice—if little Mr. Carlsson wasn't exactly what he'd claimed to be. They'd found me stupid and harmless enough to let live, while Sara Lundgren had been killed. The difference was, presumably, that they had no further use for her, while they needed me for something.

I still didn't know with certainty what that something was. However, if yesterday was a reliable indication, I was

going to be taking a lot of pictures in this northern country
—and I was going to be taking them under the very close
supervision of a young lady whose motives weren't exactly clear, to put the matter with the greatest charity
possible. It seemed just as well to make reasonably sure of
retaining control of my pix until I could determine that
everything I'd been told to photograph was completely
innocuous. Not that it had much bearing on my primary
job—Mac wouldn't give a damn what happened to my
films—but I do take a certain pride in my photography,
and I wasn't going to let it be used, unnecessarily, for
purposes of which I didn't approve.

Finished, I crossed the hall and knocked on Lou's door.
"I'm going downstairs," I called. "See you in the dining
room."

"All right, darling."

The endearment made me feel like a calculating and
suspicious beast, but one of the things you have to keep in
mind in this work is that what happens in bed, no matter
how pleasant it may be, has no bearing on what happens
anywhere else. A woman may be sweet and wonderful under
those circumstances, and still be dangerous as a rattlesnake
with her clothes on. Cemeteries are full of men who forgot
this basic principle.

When I crossed the small lobby, there was a girl speaking
to the clerk at the desk. My interest in stray females was
at a low ebb that morning, for reasons both emotional and
glandular, and this one was wearing pants—bright plaid
pants at that—so I didn't even bother to examine her
rear view closely as I headed for the dining-room door.
Her voice caught me by surprise.

"Good morning, Cousin Matthias."

I swung around to face Elin von Hoffman. That kid
could do the damndest things to herself and still be beautiful. This morning, in the loud pants and a heavy gray ski
sweater, without a trace of makeup besides that lousy
lipstick she'd worn the night before, she was still something to make you weep for your wasted life. She held out a
small key by its tag and chain.

"I brought your car," she said. "Those old Volvos are
not much good, are they?"

"It runs," I said. "What do you expect for thirty crowns
a day, a Mercedes 300SL?"

"Oh, you know sports cars?" she asked. "In Stockholm

I have a Jaguar, from Britain. It is very handsome and exciting. I also have a little Lambretta which is much fun. That is a motor scooter, you know."

I said, "Yes. I know."

She laughed. "I am still trying to educate you, aren't I? Well, I must go."

"I'll drive you," I said.

"Oh, no. That is why I came, for the walk back. I love walking, and it is such a fine day."

"It looks kind of gray and windy to me."

"Yes," she said. "Those are the best."

So she was one of the rain-in-the-face kids. Well, she'd outgrow it; she had plenty of time. I said, "That's a matter of taste. Like walking."

"You say you like hunting. If you hunt, you must walk."

"I'll walk if I can't get a horse or a jeep," I said. "I don't mind a little hike, if there's a chance of a shot at the end of it. But not just for the sake of hiking."

She laughed again. "You Americans! Everything must show a profit, even walking. . . . Good morning, Mrs. Taylor."

Lou had come down the stairs, in her working uniform of skirt and sweater and trench coat. Beside the taller, younger Swedish girl in her outdoor clothes, she looked surprisingly slight, almost fragile, although I had good reason to know that she didn't break easily. The thought, for some reason, was a little embarrassing at the moment. I saw the kid look from Lou to me and back again. She was young, but not that young; she saw something and understood it. I guess it usually shows, except on the really hardened sinners, which we were not. When Elin spoke again, there was noticeable stiffness in her voice.

"I was just leaving, Mrs. Taylor," she said. "Good-bye, Herr Helm. Your car is in the parking space across the street."

We watched her go out the door into the gray fall morning. The wind caught her hair as she came outside, and she brushed it out of her face, and tossed it back with a shake of her head, and went out of sight with the efficient, no nonsense stride of the practiced foot traveler, that you hardly ever see in America nowadays. Come to that, America never was much of a country for walkers and runners, at least after the frontier hit the Great Plains. There was just too damn much ground to cover efficiently on foot. Most of the old-timers sensibly preferred to ride. There are some real fancy foot pilgrimages on record, but if you check closely you'll find that in almost every case they start with a horse getting killed or stolen. Walking for fun is strictly a European custom.

"Who *is* that overgrown child?" Lou asked as we went on into the dining room. "I never got her name straight last night."

"Child yourself, honey bunch," I said. "From my advanced age, twenty-two doesn't look much younger than twenty-six."

"Well, you ought to know, grandpa," she said, smiling. "You were right in there looking, at dinner last night."

I seated her at a table by a window. "My interest was purely aesthetic," I said firmly. "I was admiring her as a photographer. You must admit she's so beautiful it hurts."

"Beautiful!" Lou was shocked. "That gawky—" She stopped abruptly. "Yes, I see what you mean. Although I don't go for the nature-girl type myself." She grimaced. "You hear about Sweden being such an immoral country; how do they manage to grow up with that damn dewy look? I never looked like that, and I can tell you, I was innocent as hell practically to the day I married."

"Practically?" I said.

She smiled at me across the table. "Don't be nosy. If you must know, Hal and I anticipated the ceremony slightly. As he put it, you wouldn't buy a car without driving it around the block, would you?"

"Nice, diplomatic Hal," I murmured.

She said, "Oh, I didn't mind. I . . . learned a lot from Hal. He was pretty conceited, sometimes, and he couldn't always be bothered with being kind, but we both knew he needed me. He was a strange person, very brilliant, but temperamental and erratic. Sometimes I wondered if . . . you know, I wasn't quite sure that I really meant anything to him except, well, a convenience. But you can forgive a man a great many things, Matt, when the last thing he does, with a machine gun spitting in his face, is to turn and do his best to protect you with his body. He saved my life, remember that."

She was very intent, very serious, and I knew she was trying to tell me something important. "I'll remember it," I said. "And I'll make no more derogatory remarks about Mr. Taylor. Okay?"

Lou smiled quickly. "I didn't mean to sound as if. . . . Well, maybe I did." She brought out her long cigarette holder, loaded it, and applied a match before I could act like a gentleman. "Now," she said, "you tell me about your wife and we'll have all that out of the way."

I glanced at her. "I never told you I had a wife."

"I know you didn't, darling. It was very deceitful of you, but I already had the information. You have a wife and three children, two boys and a girl. Your wife is getting a divorce in Reno on the grounds of mental cruelty, after fifteen years of marriage. It certainly took her a long time to discover that you're a brute."

I said, "Beth is a nice, sweet, bright, somewhat inhibited New England girl. She thinks wars are fought by brave men in handsome uniforms, engaging each other in open combat according to the rules of civilized warfare and good sportsmanship. Even so, she thinks it's dreadful. She was very glad that I'd spent the war behind a desk in a public information office and hadn't killed anybody. That was the story I told around, under orders. When she learned it wasn't the truth, she couldn't make the adjustment. I wasn't the same person; I wasn't the man she'd married. I wasn't even anybody she'd want to marry. There was nothing left but to call it a day." I glanced out the window, and saw with relief that our transportation was outside. The conversation had been getting slightly personal. "Finish up your coffee quick," I said. "Our escort is waiting."

I used more color on the job today because of the bad light. Black-and-white depends largely on highlights and shadows, not only for effects, but even for sharp details. On a cloudy day, it's hard to get useful black-and-white shots of intricate industrial subjects, particularly with a small camera that, necessarily, doesn't yield the ultimate in sharpness. Color, on the other hand, is almost easier to handle on a cloudy day than otherwise, since it doesn't tolerate or require strong contrasts of light and shade. With color, the colors themselves provide the necessary contrasts. If you don't insist on gaudiness, you can get some wonderful color stuff under lousy weather conditions.

We had a little rain, but not enough to drive us to cover; and we finished up around two o'clock without having stopped to eat. I spent the ride back to town worrying about the tipping problem, and settled by shaking hands with Lindström, our young guide, and thanking him for

95

all his trouble. Then I slipped the middle-aged driver five crowns, the equivalent of a buck, which didn't seem to excite him tremendously, but he didn't throw it away, either.

"Let's get something to eat uptown," I said to Lou after we'd hauled my stuff up the stairs. "I'm getting kind of tired of the hotel food."

"All right," she said, "just give me a couple of minutes to change my socks and scrape the mud off my shoes."

I went into my room to wash up—also to perform my little switch routine with the day's films. Then I went out to the car. I never like to drive a car that's been standing around, while I'm on a job, without first giving it a quick inspection, and this one had spent the night far from home.

The Volvo was standing in the hotel parking space with nothing but somebody's Triumph motorcycle for company. I walked around the little sedan once and looked inside; it was empty except for a rug or blanket provided by the management, which had slid off the rear seat onto the floor. I decided to take a chance on the doors; generally, if they have the vehicle booby-trapped, they prefer to let you get inside before they blow you up, since the explosion has a better crack at you in a confined space.

Nothing happened when I opened the door. I got the hood open. The little four-cylinder mill looked all right to me. There didn't seem to be any unnecessary wiring around the starter or its switch. I crouched to look underneath for signs that the brakes had been tampered with. There weren't any, but something was dripping out of the differential housing.

I went around to the rear and held my hand under the drip and brought it out again. The stuff wasn't any legitimate lubricant I'd ever met. It was thin and bright red like blood. Still crouching there, frowning, I saw that the source of it wasn't the differential housing at all. The stuff came from farther forward. It was dripping through the floor boards of the car onto the drive-shaft and running back. . . .

Chapter Eighteen

HE WAS LYING on the floor of the car, in the narrow space between front and rear seats, with his arms locked tightly across his stomach. I'll admit I didn't recognize him instantly. Curled up like that, he wasn't showing much of his face, and it had been a long time since I'd known him well. He was dressed in rougher clothes than those he'd worn to visit my Stockholm hotel room, the night Sara Lundgren had been killed. But it was Vance, all right. I'd have thought him dead when I removed the blanket and saw him there, except that blood doesn't usually run with any enthusiasm out of a dead body—once the heart stops pumping, there's nothing to make it run except gravity.

I tried to reach a wrist to check the pulse, but he wouldn't let himself go. I guess he had the usual gut-shot man's conviction that those arms were all that was holding him together. Maybe he was right. Whoever had done the job had certainly got him there more than once.

"Vance," I said. "Vance, this is Eric."

I thought he didn't hear me; then his eyelids fluttered. "Excuse . . . the hemorrhage," he whispered. "Very embarrassing. . . ."

"Yeah," I said. "Let's get you to a hospital. You can crack wise there."

He shook his head minutely. "No time . . . drive me where . . . talk. . . ."

I said, "The hell with talk. Just hang on while I find out where to take you in this town."

"Eric," he said in a stronger voice, "I want to report. I've been waiting several hours, hoping you'd come before . . . before. . . ."

"All right," I said. "Report, damn you, but make it fast."

"The fiancé," he whispered. "Named Carlsson. Much busi-

97

ness on Continent. Raoul Carlsson. Little man—"

I said quickly, to save his strength: "Pass the description. I've met the gentleman. What did you find out about Wellington?"

If he had to tell it, the stubborn dope, I could at least hurry him through it. But he didn't seem to hear me. He was off on another tack.

"Under no circumstances take action," he breathed. "This is an order. This is an order. The soft, peaceful sheep in Washington! How can a man defend himself, if he is forbidden to kill? He was as slow as molasses in January. Fine old American expression, eh? Did you know I've never been back to the States since the war? Always some new job, some new place. Slow as. . . . I shot him in the shoulder. All I could do, with those orders. Bah! He laughed and gave me this. Under no circumstances. . . . Why not simply order us to commit suicide?"

"Who was it?" I asked. "Who got you, Vance?"

He shook his head. "Nobody. Just a nobody with a gun. Waste no effort on him. Just put another one into Caselius for me, when the time comes." He frowned painfully. "Forgetting something. Oh, Wellington. You wanted to know about Wellington. . . ."

"Never mind Wellington," I said. "We've got to get you to a doctor now."

"No," he breathed. "No. Important. Must tell you about Wellington. Watch out for . . . Wellington is. . . ." He drew a long breath, and suddenly his eyes opened wide and he smiled a brilliant, bloody smile. "It is too bad, Eric. Now we will never know."

"Know what, Vance?"

"Know if you could . . . take me. . . ."

Then he was dead, with his wide-open eyes staring past me, seeing nothing, probably, although I can't guarantee that, never having been there. Scratch Vance, a brave man who'd made his last report, not quite complete. It occurred to me I didn't even know his real name. I got up and looked at my hands. They were red. Well, people don't usually bleed any other color.

I heard footsteps in the gravel behind me, and turned to see Lou come running from the hotel.

"What is it, Matt?" she called. "You look so. . . . What's the matter?"

I walked slowly to meet her. She stopped before me, panting from the run. I said, "There's a dead man in the car. We'll have to notify the police."

"A dead man?" she cried. "Who? Matt, your hands—"

She tried to pass me, to look, but I put myself in front of her. I said, "I'm protecting you from a horrible sight, Lou. Turn and walk into the hotel ahead of me."

"Matt—"

"Give me an argument, doll, and I'll kick your teeth in. Turn and walk. He was a good man. He doesn't want trash like you near him." She got pale and started to speak and changed her mind. She turned slowly and walked toward the hotel. Walking behind her, I said, "You'll forget I said anything to indicate I knew him."

"Yes."

"He's a perfect stranger to both of us. We have no idea how he came to be in the car. We haven't used the car since yesterday evening. It was left at *Direktör* Ridderswärd's overnight. Don't forget to bear down heavy on the title. It was driven here this morning by *Fröken* Elin von Hoffman—"

"You want me to say that?"

"Why not?"

"I thought you liked the girl."

"Like? What's like got to do with anything? I like you. Not very much right now, but I'll get over it. But I'll slit your throat at the first opportunity if you say one thing out of line; and if you think that's a figure of speech, honey, just remember what I carry in my pocket and what my business is, and think again."

She said, "Take it easy, Matt."

I said, "Use the names. Ridderswärd. Von Hoffman. Honest, upright Swedish citizens. Maybe. Anyway, it'll confuse the issue. And just keep clearly in mind that right now I'd just love to put my gory hands about your pretty neck and strangle hell out of you."

She said, "I didn't kill him, darling."

"No," I said grimly. "You have an alibi, if it happened last night, don't you, sweet?"

She looked around, shocked, and said quickly, "You don't believe—"

"Why not?" I said. "You went out into the night to get your instructions. You came back and followed them, no

99

doubt, to the letter. It's very convenient, isn't it, that we've hardly been out of each others' sight since midnight."

She said, "Darling, I swear I had no idea—"

"Yes," I said, "and you do swear real pretty, doll. And he probably wasn't shot as long ago as last night, but they'd have you take the precaution of getting an alibi, anyway, not knowing exactly when their killer would make his touch. Or maybe you call it a hit, like the syndicate boys back home. But in our outfit we call it a touch. I hope to make one soon, myself."

I drew a long breath. "Well, looking at it objectively, we're in pretty good shape. You know I didn't do it, and I know you didn't do it—not personally, at least. And the company people have had us both in sight all day, thank God. But I think you know who did it. At least you know who's responsible. Don't you?" She didn't answer. "Well, there you are," I said. "A man's been shot to death, but I don't hear you volunteering the description, name, and present address of the murderer. . . ."

The Kiruna police were polite and efficient. They were represented by a nameless officer in uniform and a plainclothes gentleman named Grankvist, whose exact status nobody bothered to explain. He was one of those lean, wiry, bleached-out Swedes. Even his eyebrows and lashes were pale, over pale blue eyes. There was a hint of something military in the way he stood and walked, but then, they've got conscription in that country, and every adult male has been exposed to a certain amount of drill and discipline.

We were questioned thoroughly and asked to present ourselves at *poliskontoret* in the morning, which we did. Here our statements were taken, signed, and witnessed, and we were told that we were free to go. Herr Grankvist himself drove us back to the hotel.

"I am sorry that you have been caused inconvenience by this unfortunate affair," he said as he let us out. "I regret that we must keep the car in which the body was found a little longer. Its condition would hardly contribute to pleasant motoring, in any case. But if another car is required, arrangements could be made—"

I said, "No, just return it to the man from whom I rented it, if you don't mind. Tell him that I'll settle with him when I return to Kiruna next week. We've decided to take the train—that is, if it's all right for us to leave town."

He glanced at me in surprise. "But of course. Everything is all cleared up, as far as you're concerned, Herr Helm. It was obviously just an unfortunate chance that caused the poor dying man to seek refuge in your automobile."

He was a little too smooth, a little too polite, a little too reassuring; and when a foreigner speaks to you in English you can never be quite sure which of his inflections are deliberate and which are a matter of accent and accident. We watched him drive away.

Lou said thoughtfully, "Well, there's a little man who isn't exactly what he seems."

"Who is?" I asked. "Come on. If we pack in a hurry, maybe we can catch the ten o'clock train out of here before he changes his mind."

I turned toward the hotel doorway, but she didn't move at once.

"Matt," she said.

"Yes?"

"You were kind of rough yesterday. I didn't mind at the time, because you'd obviously had a shock, but now you might say you're sorry."

I looked at her and remembered certain things about her —the kind of things you remember about a woman to whom you've made love. "I might," I said. "But I'm not going to."

She made a little face. "Like that, eh?"

"Like that," I said. "Do you want to come along and help me shoot these pix of yours, or would you prefer to stay in Kiruna and sulk?"

There was color in her face, and her eyes were hot and angry, but the advantage was all mine and she knew it. She had to come with me. She had to supervise the taking of the pictures. If I'd had any doubts on that score, the way she swallowed her temper and managed to smile would have settled them for good.

"Just forget I brought it up," she said lightly. "You're not losing me that easily, Mr. Helm. I'll be on the platform in ten minutes."

Chapter Nineteen

I REALLY had to hand it to the girl. Her motives might be questionable, her morals might leave something to be desired—not that I was in a position to criticize on that score—and her eye for pictures, while accurate, wasn't characterized by much in the way of freshness and originality, but her talent for organization was awe-inspiring.

Usually, on a job like that, you spend half your time waiting for somebody to find a key to unlock a gate, or for somebody's secretary to get back from a two-hour cup of joe so she can tell you the big boy's left for the golf course and you'd better come back in the morning. There was no such monkey business here. Everywhere we came, they were expecting us; and I'd be led straight to the battlefield, aimed in the right direction, and told to commence firing.

In Luleå I thought she was going to spoil her perfect record. One morning, a polite but firm young lieutenant in the off-green uniform of the Swedish Army had come up to inform us that we were operating inside the military protection district of Boden's fortress—that same mysterious fortification that had caused our airliner to make a detour the week before. In this district aliens weren't even supposed to wander from certain designated public roads and areas, let alone set up enough photographic equipment to film a Hollywood super-colossal and proceed to make a careful documentary record of freight yards and docks.

Lou smiled prettily and displayed some official-looking papers, and the boy wavered and asked our pardon. But he had his instructions, and while everything was undoubtedly in perfect order, he would appreciate our accompanying him while he checked with his superiors.

We were working to a pretty tight schedule at the time, cleaning up this eastern end of the job so we could head back to Kiruna, our headquarters, and work our way from there across the mountains to Narvik, in Norway. Any delay that particular morning would have scrambled our connections badly. Lou smiled at the boy again, and suggested he use a nearby telephone first, and call *Överste* Borg. . . .

"How the hell did you manage that?" I asked, after the kid lieutenant had departed, with apologies. "I was all resigned to bars at the windows. Who's *Överste* Borg?"

"Colonel Borg?" she said. "Oh, he's an old friend of Hal's. His wife's a darling. They had me to dinner when I was here a few weeks ago. Come on, let's finish up; we've got a plane to catch."

It seemed as if the entire north of Sweden and substantial portions of Norway were populated by old friends of Hal's, usually in fairly high official positions, all with darling wives. It made life very simple for a hard-working photographer. I asked no questions. I just went where I was led and did as I was told. It was a week to the day after Vance's death that we wrapped up the job and took the afternoon train out of Narvik, which brought us into Kiruna Central Station on time at nineteen forty-five—a quarter of eight, to you. All official times in Sweden are given on the twenty-four-hour system, as in the armed forces back home. This saves a lot of A.M.'s and P.M.'s in the railroad time tables.

In my hotel room—the same one I'd kept right along—I changed to more respectable clothes. Our old friends the Ridderswärds were having us to dinner again. Waiting for Lou to let me know she was ready to go, I organized my films and equipment for, presumably, the last time on this particular jaunt. Then she knocked on the door and came in carrying her coat, purse, and gloves in one hand, and holding up her dress with the other.

"The damn zipper's stuck," she said. "Why does it always have to happen when I'm in a hurry?"

She deposited her belongings on a chair and turned her back to me. It was the same smoothly fitting black dress she'd been wearing for important occasions right along, but it always gave me a funny feeling to see it these days, although it showed no signs whatever of the early-morning horseplay in which it had once figured. She'd got the cloth jammed in the machinery. It didn't take me long to worry loose the zipper. As a married man of fifteen years' stand-

103

ing, I'm officially checked out on zippers, single-engine, multi-engine, and jet.

I closed her up the back and gave her a brotherly pat on the fanny. We hadn't officially forgiven each other yet, but two reasonably intelligent people, reasonably equipped with senses of humor, can't work together for a week without coming to some sort of tacit understanding. I might as well have saved the pat, however. For kicks, you might as well pat Joan of Arc in full armor, as a modern woman in her best girdle.

"All clear," I said. "I asked the desk to call a taxi. It's probably waiting by now."

She didn't move at once. She was looking at the dresser top, where an impressive number of film cartridges stood in neat rows, like soldiers on parade. After a moment, she glanced at me questioningly.

I said, "That's the gather, ma'am. I lined them all up there to see what they looked like. I'll wrap them up and send them out in the morning."

She looked surprised. "I thought you were going to take them to Stockholm with you."

I shook my head. "I changed my mind. Why should I take a chance on their color processing, when I know I can get a good job in New York? As for the black-and-whites, there's a lab I know that can do a better job than I can, working in a hotel sink. It'll mean a little fun with customs, I understand, but I've been told they'll let you send exposed, undeveloped film out of the country, if you merely sign your life away first."

There was a little silence. Her back was to me, but I could see her face in the mirror. It was a mean curve I'd pitched her. She'd expected those films to be lying around for several days longer. She was thinking hard. She laughed mechanically, and touched one of the cartridges.

"My God, there are a lot of them, aren't there?"

It was a typical amateur reaction. The stuff comes out of the factories by the running mile, but the amateur clings to the notion that each square inch is precious and irreplaceable. Lou still had the attitude of the box-camera duffer who keeps the same roll in the camera from one Christmas to the next. I hadn't been able to get it through her head that film, like ammunition, is expendable.

"Yup," I said, "a lot of 'em. And there ain't a cow in

104

the herd worth a plugged nickel, ma'am."

She threw me a quick, startled glance over her shoulder. "What do you mean?"

I said deliberately, "I'm speaking from the artistic and editorial point of view, of course, not the technical. We've got lots of technically beautiful negatives, but as publishable pictures go, all we've got is a bunch of corny, unimaginative junk. I think you know that."

She swung around to face me. "If you feel like that, why did you take them?" she demanded angrily. "Why didn't you tell me—"

"Lou," I said, "don't go naïve on me at this late stage in the proceedings. You've hauled me hundreds of miles and had me expose hundreds of yards of film in weird and rather dull places that had nothing much to do with the article we were supposed to be illustrating. Any time I turned aside to shoot something really interesting, something with human appeal, something a magazine might actually go for, you'd be tapping your foot impatiently and looking at your watch. Now don't give me that wide-eyed look and start asking silly questions. You know why I took your pictures the way you wanted me to. I've been waiting for a man to show. A man named Caselius. I expect him to turn up any time now, particularly if you let him know all this stuff will be leaving the country tomorrow."

She licked her lips. "What makes you think I'm in communication with this man . . . what did you call him?"

I said, "Cut it out, Lou."

"Caselius?" she said. "Why do you expect this man Caselius to come to you?"

"Well," I said, "it's just a childish theory of mine, but I have a feeling he's interested in these pix, even if no editor would look at them twice."

"What are you trying to say, Matt?"

I said, "Honey, I'm not blind, even if I act that way occasionally. Between your connections, and my bona-fide journalistic background, and our American passports—not to mention the backing of a well-known American magazine —we've bamboozled the Swedes into letting us make a nice photographic survey of the transportation facilities and natural resources of this strategic northern area. A couple of guys named Ivan wouldn't have got past the first gate, would they?"

She said, "Matt, I—"

"Oh, don't apologize," I said. "It was a bright scheme, and it worked fine. But you're lucky you got a man like me, with an ax to grind, to do your camera work. A real magazine photographer, full of artistic integrity, might have balked at being told what to shoot and how to shoot it. At least he'd have asked some embarrassing questions."

I waited. She didn't say anything. I went on: "I suppose your friends have trained intelligence specialists working in the real top-secret areas we couldn't get access to. But we've done pretty well, as far as I can judge. We've got a set of films on this country that any professional spy would be proud to send in to headquarters. Now all that remains is getting it into the proper hands. Am I correct?"

After a moment, she said, "I *wondered* . . . you're not stupid, and still you allowed yourself to be used. . . ."

"Honey," I said, "I'm not a Swede. That's one of the discoveries a man makes as he grows up: the discovery that you can have only one woman and one country at a time. Any more and life gets too damn complicated. My folks came from here, sure, but I was born in America and I'm a U.S. citizen and I have a job to do. That's plenty of responsibility for me. Let the Swedes worry about their own politics and their own security."

"What do you mean?"

"I mean," I said, "it's nothing to me who takes pictures of what in this country, Lou, or where those pictures go. Do I make myself clear?" I took her by the shoulders to emphasize my point. "What I'm driving at, Lou," I said, looking her straight in the eye, "is there are your films, right there behind you. Tell your people to come and get them. They don't have to get rough or tricky. You don't have to poison my soup or put a mickey in my drink. The pix are nothing to me. Take them and to hell with all of you. There's just one thing I want out of the deal."

When you act like a nice guy, everybody examines your motives with a microscope. When you act like a conscience-less louse, they generally take you at face value.

Lou licked her lips again. "What's that, Matt? What do you want for your films? Money?"

I said, "Folks have been known to get smacked talking like that, ma'am. . . . No, I don't want money. I just want a look, one quick look, at a man's face. Lacking that, his name will do; the name he goes under in this country. I figure I've earned that much."

"A quick look." she said tightly, "so you can kill him!"

We were suddenly a long way apart, even though my hands were still on her shoulders. I took them away.

"The man we're talking about is the man who's probably responsible for your husband's death," I said. "Why should you worry what happens to him? That is, if your husband's really dead." A funny look came briefly into her eyes and went away. She didn't speak. I went on: "Anyway, I think you know what my orders are. Until they're changed, I'm harmless. I just want to find out who the hell I'm dealing with. I'd like to get that much of the job accomplished."

I moved my shoulders. "I'm offering you a bargain. Make up your mind. I'm not asking you to set him up for me. All I'm asking is who he is. There are your films, all together for the first and maybe the last time. You can have them easy or you can have them tough. Hell, I'm just one man, doll, and my hands are officially tied. What harm can I do? Check with Caselius himself. I don't think he's scared of letting me know who he is. I think he'll agree it's a good deal for him. His identity in exchange for the pix without fuss or trouble. What does he lose?"

She said, "You'd betray a friendly country, a country from which your people came—"

"Lou," I said, "cut it out. Let's not use big words like betray. I've got a job to do. It's not my business to protect the security of the mines and railroads of northern Sweden, a neutral country that's no ally of my country—it's not even a member of the North Atlantic Treaty Organization, to the best of my knowledge. The Swedes can damn well look out for themselves. I've got a man to find. You want your films, give me my man."

"If you got other orders," she said, "would you really—"

I said irritably, "Let's not go into the morality lecture, honey. I've heard it before."

"But it doesn't make sense!" she cried with sudden vigor. "You're a . . . an intelligent person. You're even kind of . . . kind of nice at times. And still you'd hunt down a human being like . . . like. . . ." She drew a long breath. "Don't you realize that if this man Caselius is so evil and dangerous that he must be removed, there are other ways, legal ways. . . . Can't you see that by resorting to violence,

107

you just bring yourself down to his level, the level of animals? Even if you should win that way, it wouldn't *mean* anything!"

There was a change in her attitude that puzzled me, a kind of honest indignation that was incongruous and disconcerting under the circumstances. A day earlier, a few hours earlier, I'd have spent some time trying to figure it out, but it was too late now.

There comes a time in every operation when the wheels are turning, the die is cast, the cards are dealt, if you please, and you've got to carry on as planned and hope for the best. I can name you names, too many of them, of men I've known—and women, too—who died because some last-minute piece of information made them try to pull a switcheroo after the ball had been snapped and the backfield was in motion. When that point comes, to scramble the similes even further, you just take the phone off the hook and walk away from it. You don't want to hear what the guy at the other end of the line has to say. You've done your best, you've learned everything possible in the time at your disposal, and you don't want any more dope on any part of the situation, because it's too late and you can't do anything about it, anyway.

I said, "That's kind of a funny speech from you, Lou. It seems to be kind of a set speech in these parts. Sara Lundgren—I think you've heard the name—made it, too, a few minutes before your Caselius put a nice accurate burst from a machine pistol into her face and chest."

I made an impatient gesture. "What the hell makes everybody feel so damn superior to this fellow Caselius? As far as I can make out, he's a bright, ruthless guy working like hell for his country, just like I'm a bright, ruthless guy working like hell for mine. His country doesn't happen to like my country. He's responsible for the deaths of a couple of people I'd rather have seen keep on living. I've even got some sentimental objections to his methods. Therefore it's not going to grieve me deeply if I get orders to go ahead and make the touch.

"But as far as feeling superior to the guy, nuts! I'm perfectly happy to be on his level, doll. It's the level of a tough, intelligent, courageous man who could probably make a better living selling automobiles or insurance or whatever they sell in Russia, but who prefers to serve his

108

country in the front lines, such as they are today. I don't hate him. I don't despise him. I don't look down upon him, as everybody else seems to, from some kind of a higher moral plane. I'm just prepared to kill him when and if I get instructions to do so, whether it means anything or not. Meanwhile, I'd like to find out who he is."

She said, rather stiffly. "Well, you certainly won't learn it from me, Matt." She glanced at her watch, and spoke in a different tone. "We'd better hurry. The Ridderswärds were warned we'd be late, so they're holding dinner for us, but it's not very nice to keep them waiting unnecessarily."

I looked at her. She was no longer a pretty girl whose company I'd kind of enjoyed. She was somebody who had some information I wanted. There are ways of getting information out of just about anybody, if you have a big enough need and a strong enough stomach. . . .

A funny, startled look came into her eyes. She said quietly, "No, Matt. I don't think you could make me talk."

I said, "Another woman told me that once. Remind me to tell you the story some day." I picked up her coat. "Let's go."

Chapter Twenty

I ALMOST didn't recognize the von Hoffman kid, when I came into the Ridderswärds' living room. She'd pulled her hair straight back and put it up in a big knot at the back of her head. It changed the apparent shape of her face and made her look older and more adult—kind of serene and regal—but she still stuck loyally to her putrid-pink lipstick. She was wearing the gray flannel suit that's practically a daytime uniform for the Swedish women. It comes in all shapes, shades, and sizes, but the favorite model, which Elin was displaying tonight, has a short jacket and a full pleated skirt suitable for walking or bicycling. They all wear it.

It wasn't as bad on her as the shiny blue party dress or the wild plaid pants. It didn't do anything for her, but then, she didn't really need to have anything done for her. The fact that she was wearing it, instead of dressing up, indicated that this was to be a much less formal affair than the last dinner we'd attended at this house. There were no visiting directors here tonight. Clearly this was just a little private get-together in the interests of company public relations: a graceful farewell gesture toward a couple of foreign journalists who'd finished their assignment and were about to leave.

"I have written to Colonel Stjernhjelm," Elin said to me as we settled down at the table after the same old quick-and-lousy Manhattan. She said, "I wrote that you were a terrible person, a drunkard, and probably quite immoral as well." She glanced briefly toward Lou, at the other side of the table. Then she laughed quickly. "I am joking with you, Cousin Matthias," she murmured. "I wrote that you were a very nice man. I have a reply from Colonel Stjernhjelm. He is writing you directly, but in case the letter should miss you in your travels, I am to tell you that you are invited to Torsäter for the hunt next week and he is looking forward to meeting you."

"That's very nice of him," I said. "And thank you for the recommendation."

She said, "I will be there, too. If you come on Wednesday morning, we will have a day for me to show you around. Also to sight in your weapon, if you have not already done so. I have a new, light 8mm Huskvarna bolt-action rifle that I wish to try out before I use it."

I glanced at her, a little surprised. "Oh," I said, "you'll be hunting, too."

"Why, yes," she said. "As a matter of fact, we'll be hunting together, if you do not mind too much. Colonel Stjernhjelm is in charge of organizing the hunt this year, and he will be too busy to look after you properly, so he is making me responsible for you, since you are not acquainted with our customs and methods. We hunt on stand, you know, each shooter assigned to a post, and the game is driven toward the guns by *jägare* and dogs. It is very exciting when you hear the dogs approaching and know that the *älg*—moose—is close ahead of them, and you pray that they will pass your stand and not somebody else's. I hope you are a good shot on running game. So many Americans seem to practice on nothing but stationary targets, when they bother to practice at all."

I said, "I've shot at a few moving targets in my time, Cousin Elin."

She laughed. "You make yourself sound quite ancient when you speak like that. . . . We will be sharing a stand. As the guest, you will take the first shot. But do not worry. If you miss the game, I will kill it for you."

She might look like a tall and lovely young lady, but she talked like a cocky kid. "Thanks," I said dryly.

"I am a very good shot," she said calmly. "I have written Colonel Stjernhjelm that you do not much like to walk, so we will be assigned to one of the easier stands, but it is all right. We have just as good a chance there as elsewhere."

"That's good," I said. "I wouldn't want to think you'd lost any opportunities on my account."

She laughed. "Am I being terribly undiplomatic? But we do want you to enjoy this hunt, and some of the stands are far back in quite rough country. And I am afraid we do not

111

have the jeeps or horses available to which you are accustomed in your American hunting."

Her voice was a little scornful. I had a momentary impulse to invite her to come elk hunting in the high Rockies some time. After a couple of hard days in the saddle, she might change her opinion about American hunting. . . . Later in the evening, while I was talking with my host, I saw her sitting with Lou on the far side of the living room. Both girls were smiling sweetly and talking in syrupy voices that made me want to knock their heads together. I couldn't hear what they were talking about.

Riding back to the hotel, I asked Lou, "What the hell have you and the von Hoffman kid got against each other, anyway?"

Lou gave me a surprised look that wasn't as convincing as it might have been. "Got against . . . I haven't got anything against her. I just don't go for that innocent, nature-girl type. I told you so before." She glanced at me. "I'll give you a word of advice, buster. Don't get mixed up with that one." Her voice was flat.

"What do you mean?" I asked.

She didn't look at me. "Skip it," she said. "It was just a friendly warning. I just mean she's a screwball, that's what I mean. What were you two talking about at dinner, anyway, that was so fascinating?"

I said, "Well, if you must know, we were comparing the killing power of the American .30-06 cartridge, as applied to big game, with that of the European 8mm. She's a strong eight-millimeter fan, you'll be interested to hear."

"Oh, for God's sake," Lou said. "Well, I told you she was a screwball."

Then the taxi was pulling up at the hotel. I paid—I was getting quite handy with the local currency—and followed Lou inside. We climbed the stairs in silence and stopped in front of her door.

She hesitated, and turned to look at me. "Well, I guess that's it," she said. "It's been quite an experience, anyway you look at it, hasn't it?" After a moment, she said, "We really ought to have a farewell drink on it, don't you think? I've still got some bourbon left. Come on in and help me polish it off."

It wasn't very subtle. Behind me was the door to my room, and behind that door, on the dresser top, were the

112

films—if they were still there—the films I'd threatened to send off to America at the crack of dawn. I'd figured that time limit would draw some action, but I won't say I'd anticipated it would take this form.

"All right," I said. "I'll come in, but just for a minute, if you don't mind. It's been a long day."

It had been a long day, and it wasn't over yet.

Chapter Twenty-one

CLOSING the door behind me, I had the funny tight feeling you get when you know what's coming, you just don't know what she's going to insist upon in the way of suitable, civilized preliminaries. There would be preliminaries, I was sure of that. Tonight it wouldn't be the quick, casual, what-the-hell-we're-both-adults approach she'd used before. That wouldn't take up enough time.

Tonight she had to keep me busy for a while, out of that room across the hall, until somebody passed her the all-clear signal somehow. I wondered how they were going to manage that. The wrong-number trick wouldn't work here, since there were no room phones in this arctic hotel. I watched her carry her coat to the closet and hang it up. She emerged with a bottle that had a homelike American look, and gave me a quick smile.

"I'll be with you in a minute."

"No rush," I said.

She started to say something else, changed her mind, and went behind the curtain of the rudimentary bathroom in the corner for glasses and water. Waiting for her to emerge, I looked around the room. It was pretty much like mine. Being on the opposite side of the building, it didn't have a window overlooking a vista of lake and trees—as a matter of fact, it faced the railroad station—but at night with the shade pulled down the view didn't matter. Like any hotel room, it had a couple of beds for its primary pieces of furniture. These were large, old-fashioned iron bedsteads with brass knobs—wonderful old beds, really; I hadn't seen any like them in actual use since I was a boy in Minnesota, although I'd seen plenty gathering dust in junk shops and antique stores.

There was also a comfortable upholstered chair, a hard wooden one painted white, an old white-painted dresser, a couple of small tables, and a rag rug on the floor. Although rather short of facilities considered essential elsewhere, it had a pretty nice atmosphere for a hotel room; certainly it was much more pleasant and spacious than the efficient, soulless little cubicles you get for twice the price in more modern hostelries. But as I say, in just about any hotel room, you can't get away from the damn beds. I decided I'd be perverse and make the stalling she had to do as tough as possible. I walked over and sat down on the nearest bed, making the old springs creak plaintively.

She was in the bathroom for quite a while. Then she came out with a glass in each hand, looking slender and smart and attractive in her narrow, long-sleeved, low-necked black dress. It occurred to me that I could get very fond of this girl, if I let myself. You can't work with someone for a week without coming to some conclusions about her, no matter how hard you try to avoid it. There was a moment, watching her approach, when I wanted very badly to break up this crummy business with a little injudicious honesty.

All I had to do was indicate in some way that I hadn't the slightest intention of entering my own room until my presence there would embarrass nobody; that they were welcome as could be to the films on my dresser; and that there was no need whatever for her to buy them with her body. Of course, she'd have become suspicious instantly. Being as bright as the next person, or maybe a little brighter, she'd have wanted to know why I took such a casual attitude toward those all-important pix I hoped to trade for the information I needed. . . .

Nevertheless, I was tempted. I couldn't help thinking she was fundamentally a nice kid. I didn't know how she'd got mixed up in this mess, and I didn't care. If we could just get together and talk it out, instead of playing dirty games with liquor and sex, maybe we'd find that it was all a terrible misunderstanding. . . . I was getting soft. I admit it. I was just about to break down and say something naïve like: *Lou, honey, let's put our cards on the table before we do something lousy we'll both regret.* Then I saw that she had no stockings on.

She stopped before me and smiled down at me as I sat there on the big bed. "No ice, as usual," she said. "I swear to God, the next time I come across a real highball with

115

ice cubes, I'm going to take the lovely things out and suck them like candy, with tears in my eyes."

I took the drink, and glanced again at her straight white legs, innocent of nylons. She'd been wearing them earlier, of course. I'd helped zip her up the back, remember; I'd patted her fanny in a friendly way. She'd been fully dressed then, completely enveloped in the ridiculous, delicate complex of nylon and elastic that holds the twentieth-century lady together. Well, I suppose it beats nineteenth-century whalebone, at that. But she wasn't wearing it now. That was what she'd been doing behind the curtain: shedding. Now there was just Lou, naked under her party dress, with her bare feet stuck into her slim-heeled party pumps, as on one carefree, light-hearted morning a week or so ago.

It was like a kick in the teeth. She'd remembered, and carefully filed for reference, the fact that I'd once found her irresistible dressed—or undressed—a certain way. It was the one thing that had happened between us that had been wholly spontaneous and natural. Now she was deliberately using it against me.

I made myself whistle softly. I said dryly, "This is the place for the line that goes: my girdle was killing me."

She had the grace to blush. Then she laughed, set her glass aside, and smoothed the clinging black jersey down her body, watching the effect with interest.

"I'm not very subtle, am I?" she murmured. "But then, what could I have worn, of the few things I have with me, that would have been subtle enough? I didn't pack for a honeymoon, you know. Should I go back and change into my nice warm flannel pajamas?"

I didn't say anything. She glanced at me sharply. Something changed in her face. After a moment, she seated herself beside me on the bed, picked up her glass, and drank deeply.

"I'm sorry, Matt." Her voice was stiff. "I didn't mean to. . . . I wasn't trying to seduce you, damn you. I didn't think you needed it, to be perfectly honest."

I didn't say anything. It was her party.

She drew a long breath, and drank again. "I misunderstood. . . . We probably won't be seeing each other after tomorrow, unless we happen to meet in Stockholm later. When you came in here, I thought you had a sentimental good-bye in mind, if you know what I mean. I guess I've

116

made it pretty plain I had no objections." She laughed ruefully. "There's nothing more ridiculous, is there, than a woman who gets all ready to yield up her virtue, only to find she's got no takers. Sex, anybody?" She laughed again, drained her glass, and rose. "How about another drink before you go? I need a little more to drown my humiliation."

I made a show of hesitating. Then I said, "Well, all right, just one more," and emptied my glass and handed it up to her. I watched her cross the room with a slight unsteadiness that wasn't necessarily faked; we'd both had quite a bit over the course of the evening. I felt kind of mean, just sitting there like a lump and making her carry the show all by herself. But when she returned, I saw that she'd studied her appearance carefully in the mirror and decided that, for the proper inebriated, uninhibited, delicious look, she'd better muss her hair a little and pull her dress slightly askew, just enough to tease me with a bit of shoulder and a bit of breast. I didn't have to worry about her. She was a trouper.

"Tell me," she said, dropping down beside me carelessly, "tell me about that woman."

I rescued my glass from her hand before she could drench us both, as part of the act. "What woman?"

"The one who said she wouldn't tell. You said to remind you. What wouldn't she tell, and what did you do?"

"It's hardly good bedroom conversation."

Lou laughed softly, sitting close to me. "With you feeling so virtuous, what is?"

I said, "She wouldn't tell me where she was holding my youngest child, Betsy, aged two."

Lou glanced at me, startled, forgetting how drunk she was supposed to be. "Why did she have your little girl, Matt?" I didn't answer at once, and she said, "This woman . . . this woman, did you know her before?"

"During the war," I said. "We did a job together, never mind what."

"Was she young and beautiful? Did you love her?"

"She was young and beautiful. I spent a week's leave in London with her afterwards. I never saw her again until last year. You may know that some of the people who fought the war our way changed sides later, looking for the excitement they'd got used to—not to mention the crude subject of money. Nobody ever got rich, at least not legitimately, working under cover for Uncle Sam. It turned out she was one of those who changed sides. She needed some help with a job she was on for the other team. She had Betsy kidnaped to make me co-operate."

"But you didn't co-operate? Not even with your little girl's life at stake?"

"Don't give me credit for too much patriotism," I said. "You just never get anywhere letting yourself be black-mailed, that's all. To get Betsy back on her terms, I'd have had to kill a man for her; and even then I'd have had no assurance that she'd play it straight."

Lou said, "So you tried to force the information from her. And she said she wouldn't tell."

"She said that," I said. "But she was wrong."

There was a little silence. Outside the hotel, the town was quiet. It wasn't much of a town for traffic, particularly at night.

"I see," Lou murmured. "And you got your child home safely?"

"The forces of law and order were very efficient, once they knew what address to be efficient at."

"And the woman?" She waited for my answer. I didn't say anything. Lou shivered slightly. "She died?"

"She died," I said evenly. "And my wife came walking into the place right afterward, although I'd warned her that the less she knew the better she'd like it." I grimaced. "It was a traumatic experience for her, I guess."

"I should think so!"

I glanced at Lou irritably. "Traumatic, shaumatic! It was her child, too, wasn't it? Did she want Betsy back or didn't she? It was the only way of doing it. But the way Beth started pussy-footing around me afterward, you'd think I slipped out three evenings a week to carve up women for kicks."

There was another silence. Lou drank from her glass, holding it with both hands and staring down into it. It was empty again. So was mine, somehow. Her weight was against me now, as we sat there on the big bed. She'd kicked her shoes off for comfort, and her bare feet, on the rag rug, looked more naked and immodest than her half-exposed breast. I hated her. I hated her because, despising the whole obvious business, I still couldn't keep myself from wanting her badly, just as she'd planned from the start. It had been very neat, the way she'd brought up the subject, laughed at herself, and dismissed it. She'd put a nice reverse twist on the old seduction scene, but the plot and characters remained the same. Well, I'd played coy long enough.

I said, deliberately, "I suppose, like my wife, you couldn't bear to have me touch you now, after hearing that story."

She hesitated. Then she reached out quickly and took my hand and put it to her breast. It was a beautiful and touching gesture, something to bring tears to your eyes, except for that brief hesitation, that moment of calculation, that spoiled it completely.

I said, "You sweet goddamn little phony!" and pulled her to me hard.

I kissed her, brutally, until she gasped and turned her face away. Then the full charge of anger hit me, and I wanted to hurt her worse, to strike her—and I couldn't do it. I was really pretty drunk, I guess, but something kept whispering: *go easy, go easy, watch out, you know too many ways of killing people to horse around like this.*

I couldn't get away from that nagging whisper, but I could drag the dress from her shoulder roughly, remembering how concerned she'd always been about the precious garment. I could kiss her contemptuously on the neck and shoulder and bare arm and breast, forcing the cloth downward, feeling it stretch to its limits of elasticity and beyond. She caught at my wrist in protest as sleeve and bodice tore. To hell with her. I could play as dirty as anybody. She was just a lousy little amateur; she shouldn't have tried it on an expert.

My fingers brushed the ornate bunch of satin at her hip, slick and stiff and cold to the touch after the warm wool jersey. I suppose every man has known a stray impulse to give a good yank to one of those elaborate rustling structures of satin or taffeta with which women like to call attention to their hips and rear ends. Tonight I gave the impulse free rein, and the stuff came unstitched, protesting shrilly. There seemed to be yards of it, and startlingly great portions of her dress came with it; I heard her gasp as she felt it disintegrate about her. She stopped fighting me and lay passive as I got a fresh grip on what remained, preparing to strip her completely. . . .

Then, lying there together like that, sprawled across the

119

big iron bed, breathing heavily, we were both still, listening to a racketing sound outside: somebody in the railroad station had started up one of the small motorized bikes of which the Swedes are so fond. They're kind of weak in the muffler department, and you can hear them a long way off. This fellow seemed to be right under the window. He was having trouble, apparently. The thing coughed, spat, choked, and died. He kicked it again, and it caught, and he revved it up until the noise was a high shrieking whine, and I couldn't see how he could keep from losing a valve or two, except that those damn little two-cycle motors don't have any valves. Then he rode away, sputtering, leaving silence behind him.

I raised myself slightly and looked down at Lou. She had relaxed; her face showed a kind of peace under her disordered hair.

"All right, Matt," she whispered. "All right. Go ahead. You've got that much coming."

She'd promised something—implied if not spoken—and she was going to pay off, even if she'd just heard the all-clear signal and knew there was no further need to keep me occupied. Suddenly I was neither drunk nor angry. I just felt kind of foolish and ineffectual, stopped in the middle of ripping the clothes off a woman I couldn't bring myself to hurt and didn't, I realized, particularly want to rape. I mean, sex shouldn't be a weapon, an instrument of hate. It's something you share with a woman you like. At least you can try to keep it that way.

I got up slowly, and looked at her lying there across the bed, tangled in some inadequate wreckage that no longer bore much resemblance to clothing. I found myself, for some reason, remembering how Sara Lundgren had looked after Caselius and his boys got through with her. Well, at least Lou was still alive; and I'd never claimed that Caselius and I weren't pretty much on the same level, morally speaking. It remained only to see which of us was tougher, which was smarter.

I started to say something bright and clever, and stopped. Then I started to say something apologetic, which was even sillier. It wasn't a time or place for speeches, anyway. I just turned and walked out of the room.

Chapter Twenty-two

IN THE HALL outside my room, I had the key in the lock. I was ready to push the door open and step inside, when it occurred to me that was the way people went and got themselves killed. They got themselves all upset about a woman or something, and forgot to take stock of a changed situation that might hold danger.

If everything had gone according to plan, my situation had changed drastically—at least Caselius would be thinking it had, which was what counted—and I remembered very clearly what had happened to Sara Lundgren when our boy decided he had no further use for her.

I reached in my pocket, got the Solingen knife, and flicked it open. Standing aside, I gave the door a push and waited for it to swing all the way back. Then I waited a little more. If there was anyone inside, he could watch that lighted dorway for a while and wonder whether the first object through would be a human being or a hand grenade. It would do his nerves good, from my point of view.

When I went in, I went in fast and low, at a slant. It would have taken a very good man to pick me off in the brief moment I was silhouetted against the light. I hit the floor inside and kept rolling, and nothing happened. You feel kind of silly, getting yourself bruised and dusty for nothing, but it's better than being dead. I lay there in the dark long enough to decide that if I wasn't alone in the room, the other guy must have passed out from holding his breath. Then I got up and moved cautiously to the window to pull the blind, keeping well to one side, before I turned on the light. I didn't look out. A white face makes a swell target, and I wasn't curious. If there was a sniper outside, that was a good place for him to be. He didn't bother me a bit, out there.

With the window safely covered, I went back and closed

the door and hit the light switch. The Swedes go in for large push buttons, like overgrown doorbell buttons. You hit them once for light, and once again—the same button —for darkness. Then I looked at the dresser top, which was empty. The films were gone. The surprise wasn't exactly what you'd call paralyzing.

I went behind the bathroom curtain and looked at myself in the mirror. I had a streak of her lipstick across one cheek and more on my shirt collar; I had her face powder on my lapels. I had some scratches on my wrist where she'd tried to hold me off. Otherwise she'd done me no visible harm. Damage-wise, as the Madison Avenue boys would say, it had been strictly a one-way proposition.

My image in the mirror had that dead-fish look that your mirror image always gets after you've drunk too much. I was beginning to need a shave, I noticed. I needed a bath. I needed a good beating-up or the firm application of an old-fashioned horsewhip. I needed a new face and a new personality. I needed twelve hours' sleep.

I settled for washing my face and taking some aspirin. When someone knocked on the door, the sound was barely audible, but it made me jump a foot. I took out the knife again and went to the door and opened it, taking the routine precautions. Outside was the last person in the world I expected to see right then. You'd have thought she'd had enough of me for a while. I folded the knife and put it away. It was getting lots of fresh air tonight, but no exercise.

"Come in, Lou," I said. She didn't move at once. She was watching my face. "Yes," I said, "your friends have been here. Congratulations."

She drew a deep breath. "Matt, I—"

"Come in," I said. "It's safe. I never maul the same woman twice in one night."

She stepped inside. I closed the door and turned to look at her. She'd done a quick restoration job; you wouldn't have known this was a girl I'd just left lying across her bed in rags. She had her old beatnik costume on—the tight black pants, the bulky black sweater—and her hair was brushed and her lipstick was bright and straight. There was a small red area on her chin, that was all.

We faced each other in silence; then I said, "Everything okay?"

She nodded. "Yes," she said. "I . . . I'm all right."

I reached out and touched the mark on her chin. "Whisker burns?" She nodded again. I said, "I'll have to remember to shave for the next young lady I ravish."

She said, "You didn't finish ravishing this one, Matt." There was a spell of silence. She said, "It wasn't . . . wasn't very nice, what I had to do to you, what we did to each other. I don't blame you for hating me and wanting to hurt me."

I didn't want her damn understanding. "That's nice of you," I said. "I appreciate that."

She shook her head quickly. "Don't be sarcastic, please. Some day, maybe soon, you'll understand why. . . ." Her voice ran out. After a little, she said, "If there's anything . . . anything I can do to make up for tricking you. . . ."

I said, "I figured we came out pretty even."

She glanced toward the empty dresser top. "Still?"

"Still," I said.

She grimaced. "I don't seem to have much luck selling myself tonight, do I?"

"Oh, is that what you were doing?" I asked. I looked her up and down briefly. "Well, I never could get excited over a woman in pants, doll."

She said, completely without expression: "That's easily remedied. They come off, you know."

It was no use. I couldn't out-tough her. I admitted defeat. "Let's cut it out, Lou. I've had just about enough of this smart-and-dirty dialogue."

She said, stiffly, "I just don't want you to feel . . . well, cheated. At least not in that way. And I don't want you to feel noble and forgiving, either. I want to have all our accounts settled when I go out of here. We probably won't meet again. If you think you've got something coming, damn you, now's the time to collect." Then she started to cry.

After a little, I got a clean handkerchief from my suitcase and gave it to her. She wiped her eyes and blew her nose and looked at the handkerchief in a baffled way.

"Keep it for a souvenir," I said. "When you look at the discreet monogram, in the years to come, remember me."

She stuck it into her pants pocket. "Well, I seem to have finally succeeded in making a complete sap of myself," she said. "I guess it's time to go."

She turned away. I let her get as far as the door. Then I said, "Lou."

She turned to look at me. "Yes?"

"A message," I said. "From one M. Helm to one X. Caselius, if you should happen to encounter the gentleman."

Her eyes widened slightly. "What's the message, Matt?"

I said, "I offered you a deal, remember? You turned it down."

"I remember."

I said, "Well, if Massa Caselius should be in any way dissatisfied with the films you-all went to so much trouble to get tonight, honey, you just whisper in his ear that I might be able to help him out. There's only one catch. He'll have to come in person. I still have a downright yearning to see his face."

She was staring at me, wide-eyed, with a look of shock and horror. "Oh, *no!*" she whispered, as if to herself, and then to me: "Oh, you fool! You stupid, meddling *fool!* How *could* you—"

Her voice caught on a sob. She whirled and snatched at the door handle in a blind sort of way, got the door open, and ran out. I heard the scuffing sound of her soft shoes go down the hall fast.

After a moment, I shrugged and went after her. I was a success. I'd got a great big reaction. I'll be honest and admit I didn't know why. I went after her to find out. She was turning down the stairs as I came into the hall. I heard her stop halfway down. I went as far as the corner and took a cautious look.

From the head of the narrow stairs you looked right down into the lobby. Actually, it was little more than a vestibule, with just room enough for people to transact their business at the desk and hang up their coats on the way to the dining room. This limited space, I saw from my point of vantage, was rapidly becoming occupied by cops and other people, just as fast as they could get in the door. Halfway down the stairs, pressed against the wall, was Lou, staring down at this influx of law-enforcement talent.

When she came out of her trance and tried to flee, it was too late. One of the policemen had spotted her and pointed her out to Grankvist, our blond friend with the pale eyebrows. He was fast on his feet. He came up those stairs like a man in first-class condition. She missed a step in her haste, coming back up toward me; she went to one knee. Before she could recover, Grankvist had her.

Surprisingly, she gave him a fight. He was just a poor damn government employee doing his duty, but she gave him the battle that, with much more provocation, she hadn't given me. He got thoroughly bitten and scratched, and two tall policemen had to give him a hand, before he got her subdued.

I'd been too busy watching the ruckus and keeping in the shadow and out of sight—they'd been pretty close to me—to pay much attention to what was going on below. Now, as Lou was hauled down the stairs, I saw a familiar figure down there. They grow Swedes tall, but they don't generally grow them very wide. This man was both tall and wide. He crowded that little vestibule just by being in it.

"I see you've got her," he said in English to Grankvist.

"Yes, Herr Wellington," said the blond man, patting his scratched face with a handkerchief. "We have her. But the next time we work together for the good of our respective countries, may I suggest that *you* take the woman?"

Wellington laughed. "I warned you she'd be a wildcat." He gestured toward the door. "Our part of the operation went like clockwork. We caught him with the photographs in his possession, all legal and proper. Herr Grankvist, may I present Herr Caselius?"

I looked toward the door. The dapper small figure was practically invisible in that room jammed with tall men; but I had reason to remember a deserted road and a swift blade. Unlike Lou, the little man had apparently allowed himself to be taken without a struggle. He looked neat and serene between his police guards, and the pin in his tie reflected the light brightly.

"There must be some mistake," he said calmly. "My name is Carlsson. Raoul Carlsson, of the house of Carlsson and LeClaire. . . ."

Well, I had my answer, for what it was worth. I went back to my room. They'd be coming for me soon enough, but maybe I could get some sleep first.

Chapter Twenty-three

IT WAS four in the morning when they started breaking down the door. At least it sounded like that to a man fighting his way upward out of fathoms of sleep. Everybody else had seemed to have no trouble whatever getting in and out of my hotel rooms, wherever they might be. I couldn't see why these jokers had to make such a production of it.

"This is the police." It was Grankvist's voice. "Open the door, Herr Helm."

"I'm coming," I said.

I turned on the light and glanced at the knife on the bedside table. There have been cases of people getting dead from opening the door to cops who weren't cops. But the voice was familiar and I wanted to look gentle and peaceful in the eyes of the local law. I'd finished one theatrical engagement; now I had a new role to play. I dropped the knife back into the pocket of my pants, where they hung on a chair, yawned, checked the time—that's when I learned it was four o'clock—and went over barefooted to let them in.

I turned the key in the lock. The door came back at me, knocking me off balance. I caught a glimpse of Wellington's massive shape; then his fist caught me alongside the jaw and I went sideways and down. Like I say, I never could do much with fists myself, but there are people who can.

He gave me no chance to pick myself up. He was on top of me as I got to hands and knees. He was growling like a bear. I gathered he was mad about something. I could even make a fairly accurate guess what it was. He clubbed me across the back of the head and I went down again. I had barely consciousness enough left to roll away, knowing that a kick was next. It caught me in the ribs and slammed me against the wall. That was enough. I curled

126

up and played possum. He kicked me once more and yanked me up and slapped my face a couple of times, but you don't get much of a charge from beating up a guy who apparently can't feel it. He let me go again, and I slithered artistically to the floor and stayed there with my eyes closed, thinking about the fun I'd have with him some day. I love big tough men who shove me around. They buried the last one I met with five bullets in his chest.

"You dirty renegade," Wellington was saying. "You miserable scum, to call yourself an American—"

I didn't pay much attention to him. What he said didn't matter. He wasn't going to finish me off, obviously, and that was his mistake. He got into a hassle with Grankvist, who thought he'd overdone it a bit, I guess. Finally Grankvist lost his patience.

"I am in command here, Herr Wellington!" he snapped. "Your help has been appreciated, but if you do not take control of yourself I will call the men outside and have you escorted from this room. There was no need for such violence!"

Wellington said in a sour voice, "All right, all right, I'll be good. I just wanted a couple of swings at him before you boys took over. After all the trouble we've gone to, to have it all shot to hell because of one lousy—"

"Please, Herr Wellington!" Grankvist approached and knelt beside me. "Herr Helm."

He rolled me over. I let myself come to, gradually, opening my eyes and looking up into his narrow Nordic face. I sat up and rubbed my jaw without speaking. Grankvist looked embarrassed.

"Are you all right, sir? Can you stand up?" He helped me to my feet. "It was an error on my part, I'm afraid. I misjudged the strength of Herr Wellington's feelings."

I said, "That's not the only part of Herr Wellington you misjudged the strength of. Jesus!" I glanced at the big man, and looked back to Grankvist. "What's that gorilla have against me, anyway?"

Grankvist frowned. "You ask that?"

"Damn right I ask it," I said. "I'm just a poor damn American photographer, I know, a foreigner and all that, but I was under the impression this was a peaceful and law-abiding country. So the police wake me up in the middle of the night, and I open the door, and a crazy man eight feet tall knocks me down and walks all over me!"

Wellington stepped forward. "Listen, Helm, that innocent stuff isn't going to get you—"

"Mr. Wellington, I must insist!" Grankvist held up his hand. "Let us approach this matter reasonably."

I rubbed my bruised ribs. "Let's do," I said. "It's about time. First let's get our identities straight, if you don't mind. I know who you are, Grankvist; at least you seem to have something to do with the police. Okay. But what's this guy doing here? The last I heard, he was an American businessman and an admirer of Mrs. Taylor's. Will somebody tell me what an American businessman is doing beating up people for the Swedish police? What's the matter, haven't you got anybody big enough among your own men?"

"Herr Helm—"

I turned on the anger a little more. "Look, Grankvist," I said, "I don't know what's going on here, but I do know that the American Embassy's going to hear about this business. What do you mean by busting into my room. . . ." I wheeled on Wellington, who'd started to dig through my open suitcase. "Damn you, leave my stuff alone!"

He gave a triumphant laugh, and came up with the little Smith and Wesson. "I thought so! Here, Grankvist. Would an innocent American traveler be packing a .38?"

He tossed the weapon across the room. Grankvist caught it and looked at me questioningly.

I said, "What the hell does that signify? If you want to be technical, I've got import licenses—"

"For this?" The Swede shook his head. "I doubt it, Herr Helm. We do not often permit the importation of pistols by private citizens."

I said irritably, "Well, hell, I had papers for the rifle and the shotgun; I didn't figure it would bother anybody if I tossed that pea-shooter into my baggage. I've always had a handgun around, out west where I live; I'd feel sort of naked without it."

"It's highly illegal here, I'm afraid."

"All right, so arrest me!" I said angrily. "Is that what this is all about? Two big operators in my room and God knows how many more out in the hall, a sock on the jaw and a couple of kicks in the ribs, just because I slipped a little five-shot .38 into my gear when I was packing?"

Grankvist was watching me narrowly. I sensed that behind his official calm he was just a little worried. He said, "You really claim not to know why we are here, Herr Helm?"

Wellington made a rude sound in his throat. "You're not going for that routine, are you, Grankvist?" he demanded. "This guy's obviously in cahoots with—"

Grankvist said, "Mr. Wellington! I've asked you—"

"Rats!" Wellington snorted. "He knows why we're here!" He reached into his pocket and jerked something out. It was long, wet, and black. It stuck to itself, and I didn't think it had benefited the lining of his pocket any, either. He hauled another one out of the other pocket. It was a hell of a way to carry film, but then, after what I'd done to it, the stuff wasn't much good anyway. "There!" he said, throwing the two films on the bed. "That's what we're here about, Helm! Those two and a bushel of others just like them! The military just finished developing them for us, rush. All black! Fogged! Completely blanked out, so you couldn't tell what had been on them! Useless as evidence, absolutely useless, after all the work—"

He stopped as I burst out laughing. He took a step toward me. I stopped laughing abruptly. "Come on, Large Boy," I said. "This time I'm ready for you."

"Gentlemen!" Grankvist protested.

I turned to him. "Keep this Ivy-League ape away from me," I said. "Nobody kicks me and gets away with it— but nobody. I'll settle with him one of these days. If you don't want it to be right here and now, keep him off me."

Wellington said tightly, "Don't look now, Helm, but your act is slipping. You don't sound like an innocent photographer now, to me or to Mr. Grankvist either."

I said, "You let me worry about that, partner. I've been taking care of myself a long time in a lot of rough places. I've taken pictures where you couldn't have held a camera, you'd have been kept too busy changing into dry pants. Don't you worry one little bit about me, son. Nobody's yet kicked Matthew L. Helm and got away with it, and I don't propose to let them start now." Then, as if overcome by a sudden memory, I snickered again.

Grankvist stared at me. "What do you find so humorous, Herr Helm?"

I shook my head ruefully. "I don't know what you boys

have been up to, and I'm sure sorry if I've spoiled anything for you, but I'd have liked to see the face of the man who pulled that first film out of the hypo—expecting thirty-six fine exposures of military secrets, I suppose!"

Wellington burst out, "So you admit—"

Grankvist held up his hand. "I'll ask the questions. Or perhaps it would be best if Herr Helm just told the story his own way."

I said, "It's not much of a story. Like I say, I've been taking care of myself for quite a while. She was a hell of a nice-looking girl, but she sure had gone to a lot of trouble to have everybody eating right out of her hand, and she sure was set on having just the right pictures taken just the right way, clear and sharp. After a while it became pretty damn obvious we weren't going to be selling the stuff to any magazine. It just wasn't magazine material, if you get what I mean. Well, I like to stay out of trouble. So I'd spend the day taking pictures with her, and in the evening I'd just kind of pull each film out of the cartridge and hold it under the light for a spell before I rolled it back up—"

"If that isn't the damndest story I ever heard!" Wellington snorted. "You know damn well you got wind of what we were up to and fogged the film to protect Caselius from the trap we were setting for him!"

"Caselius?" I said. "Who's Caselius?"

Grankvist said, "If you had suspicion of espionage, it was your duty to report it to the authorities."

I said, "Mr. Grankvist, with all due respect to your country, I don't happen to be a citizen of Sweden. My only duty as a guest here, as I saw it, was to make sure that my cameras and my pix weren't put to any harmful use. Well, I made sure, didn't I?"

The Swede shook his head. "It still does not seem very logical to me, Herr Helm. Why go to all the trouble of taking pictures, if you were going to destroy them the same day?"

I sighed and looked uncomfortable. "Well, now you embarrass me, son," I said. "But that was a mighty sweet little girl—I certainly hope she hasn't got herself in any bad trouble. And as long as she thought I was taking the pictures she wanted, she was real nice to me, if you get what I mean. And my wife left me some months ago, and you know how it is when a man gets used to having . . . Well, like I said, it's embarrassing. I guess you'd say I'm no gentleman, Mr. Grankvist. On the other hand, trying to trick me into taking her pictures like that, I don't think you could call her a real lady, either."

Grankvist cleared his throat. "Yes," he said. "Well, I see." Obviously he disapproved and thought I was a calculating and immoral character; and the fact that I'd willingly revealed such a reprehensible side of my nature, as always happens, inclined him toward believing in me. If I'd acted pure and virtuous, he'd have thrown me in jail. After a moment, he said: "As you've probably gathered, Mr. Wellington and I, as agents of our respective governments, have been trying to capture a certain troublesome foreign espionage agent, a man who sometimes goes by the name of Caselius. We went to considerable lengths to insure that this man would be caught with incriminating evidence upon him. Unfortunately, due to your precaution in exposing your films to light, our evidence is worthless. We've had to release the man and his female accomplice with apologies."

"I see," I said. "Well, I sure am sorry, son." I hesitated. "It's a silly question, I suppose, but why didn't you tell me what was going on? As an American citizen, I'd have been happy to co-operate."

Grankvist hesitated, and glanced at Wellington without friendliness. "The suggestion was made," he said coldly. "Mr. Wellington didn't approve it, for some reason." He cleared his throat. "I am sorry for having disturbed you, Herr Helm, and I am truly sorry for the violence that occurred, for which I must take responsibility, since I am in charge. Under the circumstances, I can hardly be legalistic about your little gun, can I? However, your possession of it is contrary to law, so I will have to confiscate the weapon temporarily. It will be returned to you when you leave this country. Is that satisfactory to you?"

We looked at each other for a moment. We understood each other. If I made no trouble about getting pushed around, he'd make no trouble about my illegal weapon. . . . On second thought, I wasn't quite sure I'd better assume that I understood him completely. He'd gone for my act just a little too quickly, and it hadn't even been one of my best performances.

"Quite satisfactory, Herr Grankvist," I said. "I'm sorry to have spoiled your plans."

He gave a shrug that was more Latin than Nordic. *"Det händer,"* he said. "It happens. Are you coming, Herr Wellington?"

"I'll be along," Wellington said, watching me.

Grankvist frowned, and looked at me quickly. I said, "It's all right. As a fellow-citizen, whose taxes presumably pay his salary, I've got a few questions to ask Mr. Wellington. I'll scream for help if he tries to bully me again."

Grankvist looked from one to the other of us, gave his shrug again, and walked out. Americans have the reputation of being crazy the world over, I guess.

Chapter Twenty-four

AFTER THE DOOR had closed behind the Swede, I got up and went to the so-called bathroom and took a couple more aspirins. When I came back, Wellington had got out a long cigar and lighted up. Back in the days when I was smoking myself, I didn't notice it so much, but now I get kind of annoyed with people who stink up the premises without so much as asking if I mind. Well, there wasn't much chance of my loving him like a brother anyway.

I pulled on a dressing gown and stuck my feet into slippers. I had a couple of very sore ribs; and chewing was going to be no pleasure for a couple of days, after that poke in the jaw. He smoked and watched me. I jerked my head toward the door through which Grankvist had gone.

"You didn't tell him everything, apparently," I said. "For one thing, he still seems to think Lou Taylor was Caselius' loyal accomplice, but she was actually working for you, wasn't she?"

He said, "I told Grankvist just what he needed to know."

"Yeah," I said. "Like you told me. What outfit do you report to, anyway?"

He named the organization readily enough. It was the same as Sara Lundgren's. I hadn't known they had two full-fledged operatives in this little country. Obviously I hadn't been supposed to know. Vance had apparently discovered it, however. It was what he'd been trying to tell me when he died.

I said, "I don't suppose I have to identify myself."

"No," he said. "We know you, you sonofabitch."

He was a real lovable specimen. I said, "You made a bobble, brother. You goofed. You got security-happy, or something, and couldn't bring yourself to confide in one of the people necessary to your scheme. You thought you could pull it off, working around me, using me, without

133

coming right out and asking for my co-operation. It's a mistake you guys often make, not trusting people. But if you don't tell them, you can't very well blame them for screwing up your plans, can you?"

He got up from the chair in which he'd been sprawled. He didn't have any height on me, but that width and weight made it seem as if he were towering over me. I estimated the position of the nerve center I intended to go for if he started to get funny again. They say you can kill a man by hitting him there hard enough. He was big enough to make it an interesting experiment.

He said, "Still acting innocent, aren't you? Well, it doesn't go, Helm. I know you. I've known about you and your hush-hush outfit for a long time. I got curious about you and your mission, that time during the war—oh, I recognized you in Stockholm, just like you recognized me—and I did a little digging around afterward and found out some interesting things. I know what you people do. I know that you generally work pretty much alone. I know you've got the reputation of being a bunch of prima donnas, although what the hell you've got to be proud of, I couldn't say!"

He was really a hell of a big guy, and somehow his conservative Harvard-Yale-Princeton clothes made him look even bigger. When the time came, I'd have to cut him down at once. He was too big to play with, although it would have been fun.

He said, "I've met some miserable, jealous, bureaucratic bastards in my time. But I've never before met one who'd deliberately spoil a job other people had worked months on, risked their lives on, just to keep it for himself!"

I stared at him. Well, these organization men judge everybody by themselves. He was just giving me credit for his own brand of thinking. He'd tried to hog the job for himself without cutting me in, and he assumed I'd acted from the same motive.

"Look," I said, "I'll tell you once more in plain language: I didn't know I was dumping anybody's apples, except perhaps Caselius'. You didn't tell me. What I want to know is, *why* didn't you tell me?"

We kicked it back and forth for a while. I won't bore you with the exact dialogue. Just figure out what the employees of two different government departments would be

134

likely to say to each other after discovering that they'd been working at cross purposes, and you'll be close enough. At the end, he was still firmly convinced that I'd fogged my negatives to spite him; and I still wanted to know why he hadn't taken me into his confidence about what he was trying to do.

At last he burst out: "Tell you? You damn butcher, after what you did in Stockholm, do you think I'd ask any help from you?"

"What did I do in Stockholm?" I asked. "Oh, you mean Sara Lundgren?"

"Damn right, I mean Sara!" he said. "Okay, so she was crazy about the guy—what the hell do they see in these slick little Continental types anyway?—but as long as she was in contact with him she was a potential gold mine to us. We just kept an eye on her and made sure she didn't slip him anything important—"

"Nothing important," I said, "except about me. She blew my cover the minute I stepped ashore."

He said, "Hell, it wouldn't have hurt you. Caselius needed an American photographer badly, too badly to quibble about whether the guy packed a gun in his camera case. Anyway, he'd have seen through your corny disguise soon enough. This way Sara got the credit for unmasking you."

"Swell," I said. "It did her a lot of good. And I don't recall anybody's consulting me."

He said impatiently, "I was pretty sure Caselius would go ahead and use you anyway. Well, he did, didn't he? He's the kind who'd actually be tickled at the thought of having an American agent do his photographing for him. He'd just take the precaution of running a few simple tests to see what kind of a guy he had to deal with, first having his boys knock you around a bit and then checking you out himself with cold steel. You assayed fairly high on stupidity, I understand. You even let him know you were pretty good with a knife, so he knew what to watch out for. He's a conceited little guy. It would give him a big kick to use and outsmart a man who'd been sent to kill him. I counted on that."

"I see."

Wellington grimaced. "What did you lose? We had to let Lundgren pass on *some* genuine information, didn't we? If he'd spotted you on his own, and she'd said nothing

135

about you, he'd have wanted to know why. We wanted her to keep her standing with the little man, so that we could use her to slip him a false lead later, if things broke that way. Afterward, she'd have been quietly shipped back to the States and eased out of the service—nobody wants the publicity of a trial, in a case like that.

"She wasn't a bad chick, you know, just a little stuck-up, too good for us crude American boys. It was good for a laugh, if your sense of humor ran that way, when a real smoothie came along and played her for a sucker. It would have been punishment enough for her to be tossed out on her ear and have to spend the rest of her life remembering what a sap the little man had made of her. But you couldn't leave it at that, could you? You had to be judge, jury, and executioner. You spotted the double-cross and lowered the boom, just like that."

I said, startled, "Hell, I didn't kill her!"

He shrugged, unimpressed. "She went into the park to meet you. You came out, she didn't. You're the big dangerous man, aren't you? Whether you killed her or just stood back and let them kill her doesn't much signify, does it? She was with you. You're the smart, tough bastard, sent out to fix things after all the rest of us poor fumbling dopes have failed. Are you going to tell me you couldn't have saved her if you'd wanted to, Superman?"

I started to speak and stopped. He was convinced. Nothing I could say was going to unconvince him. Maybe there had been a little more between him and Sara Lundgren than he'd indicated, to make him feel so strongly—or maybe he'd just have liked there to be. And after all, what he said was quite true. I'd gone to meet a woman in the park and left her there dead. It wasn't anything I could be proud of. It wasn't worth an argument. Anyway, we'd talked enough about Sara. There was another woman I was more interested in.

"Taylor?" he said when I asked. "Yes, sure she was working for me. Hell, you saw us together one night, didn't you?" I didn't say anything. I was still trying to rearrange my thinking around all this new information. He went on after a moment, "You made quite an impression on her. I guess you must be hell with women. She kept pleading with me to let her tell you what we were doing. That's why she insisted on meeting me outside here, to make her

136

pitch again, although it was risky as hell. I told her to keep her mouth shut, but obviously she decided she knew best and went against my orders."

"What do you mean?"

He said scornfully, "Oh, come off it! She must have told you what was going on. Otherwise, how could you have known enough to cut the ground right out from under us with this lousy film trick?"

I said, "She didn't tell me anything."

He shook his head, dismissing this as not even worth comment. "Let me tell you something, Helm," he said. "You may think you're going to hog Caselius and the credit for yourself, now that you've run us off the track, but you're forgetting one thing, aren't you, a little matter of orders? Sara tied a muzzle on you with that letter she wrote to Washington, didn't she? Caselius put her up to it, of course, but I didn't mind a bit. I'd asked for more time to trap him legally, co-operating with the local authorities, who didn't much like the idea of having a well-known foreign spy taking cover under a Swedish identity and Swedish citizenship. Washington wouldn't listen, until Sara wrote, as the resident agent on the spot, protesting the barbaric notion of sending a trained assassin into a friendly country, etc., etc. Then they got scared and decided to call you off and give me my chance. I was instructed—get this, Helm —I was instructed to make use of your specialized talents only if, in my considered judgment, it was absolutely necessary for the success of our mission." He grinned wolfishly. "Guess what my considered judgment is, fella. You'll grow roots like a tree, waiting for action orders from me. We'll get Caselius some way, in spite of you and without you."

"We?" I said. "You and Lou Taylor?"

His expression changed slightly. "No, I was speaking editorially, I guess. As far as Taylor's concerned, I don't figure her chances are very good. But I couldn't very well stop her, under the circumstances."

"What do you mean?" I asked sharply.

"You heard Grankvist. She went off with Caselius, when they were released. I tried to talk her out of it, but she felt she had to do it, and you can see why."

"*You* can, maybe," I said. "Brief me."

He hesitated. Then he said, "Well, the whole scheme

was pretty much her idea. She contacted our people in Berlin secretly, and they passed her on to me in Stockholm; I'd been assigned there to check up on Lundgren and take over her duties. My cover was good—Lundgren was still carrying the ball for us, as far as the other side knew—so Taylor and I just played it straight: the American businessman paying court to the pretty American widow. As far as Caselius knew, I was just another old friend of Hal's whose connections might come in handy. Of course, he knows better now. That's another strike against her, wherever she is. Anyway, whether or not he believes she double-crossed him, he knows she can't be of any more use to him, and he's not a little man to burden himself with excess baggage."

I said, "You're just a ray of sunshine, aren't you? If you can figure that out, so could she. And still she went with him?"

He shrugged. "Like I say, she felt she had to. . . . She told us the whole thing, of course, starting with that damn gaudy article her husband wrote. It was pretty much a gag, you know. There was hardly a word of truth in it. Mister Taylor had just stumbled across the name somewhere. He'd picked up a lot of stray dope about intelligence and counter-intelligence in his work. When a magazine offered him a nice fat check for a sensational article on the subject, he stuck his tongue in his cheek and started beating on his typewriter. Title: CASELIUS, THE MAN NOBODY KNOWS. Text: full of terrific facts that just didn't happen to be so. He didn't really consider it cheating, according to his wife. He just thought it was a hell of a good joke on everybody. He was that kind; he liked fooling people."

I said, "If all that's true, why was he killed?"

Wellington laughed, and walked back to the big chair and sat down. He waved his stinking cigar at me. "Look at it from Caselius' standpoint, fella. That little man's no dope. Dozens of bright operatives on our side have been trying to trap him for years. They haven't succeeded, true, but gradually they've drawn a ring around him, if you know what I mean. They've driven him from one cover to the next; now he's compromised this Swedish disguise that I figure he was more or less keeping as a last resort. And then he reads this crap about himself: Caselius, the great hulking espionage genius with a Cossack beard and a laugh that shakes the Kremlin walls. His organization's described in detail, all wrong—"

"Lundgren seemed to think he had that fairly correct."

"Sara said what Caselius wanted her to say. When these proud, independent females fall for a guy, they really fall. The article was way off the beam in practically every respect, take it from me. Caselius couldn't have asked for a more perfect red herring. All he had to do was call attention to the piece somehow, make it seem genuine.

"He's a great boy for direct action: he simply lured the author into an ambush and had him shot to pieces. That made it look as if Mister Taylor had really got hold of something, some genuine information, important enough that Caselius had to have him killed because he knew too much to live. So Hal Taylor became a martyr, and his crazy magazine piece became—in some circles, at least—the authoritative reference work on Caselius, the bearded giant, while Caselius himself went happily on his way, laughing up his sleeve, planning his next operation while he sold silly dresses to silly women in silly dress shops all over Europe—a cute little Swedish citizen not much more than five feet tall."

Wellington grimaced. "He's really a cocky little bastard. He even gave us a clue. Did you know that Caselius is simply a latinized version of Carlsson? When a Carlsson comes into money and wants to get fancy, he calls himself Caselius in this country, just like at home a Smith might get notions to call himself Smythe."

It was getting pretty thick in the room from that cigar. I glanced toward the window, and changed my mind. I didn't figure there was much danger any more, if there ever had been. By now Lou would have let Caselius know he couldn't spare me quite yet. However, timing and communications are tricky in such matters, and there was no sense in taking unnecessary chances for a little fresh air.

Wellington was waiting for me to ask a question. I fed him his line. "I still don't quite see how Lou Taylor got into the act."

Wellington said, "Well, there was just one hitch in Caselius' plans, fella. It seems that the machine gunner at that road block wasn't quite as hot with his weapon as

Caselius himself seems to be. When they got to the car, it was a shambles of course, blood all over the place, but underneath her husband's body Mrs. Taylor was still very much alive.

"And when they started hauling the body off her, they found that it wasn't quite dead, either. It was pretty badly shot up, but some guys are tough. Hal Taylor stubbornly insisted on keeping right on living. He's still over there, despite the urn of ashes and the neat little gravestone with his name on it, somewhere in France. Caselius is a thoughtful guy. He has somebody take a picture now and then for him to show to Mrs. Taylor, so she can see how her husband's coming along. Somehow, Hal Taylor's progress toward recovery seems to depend largely upon how well his wife does what Caselius asks her to. Does that clear things up for you, fella?" After a moment, he said, "I've got a couple of the pictures. Here."

He took them from his pocket. They were dog-eared snapshots, apparently taken with a cheap box camera with a flash attachment, fairly lousy in quality. One showed a bandaged man in a white hospital bed, nice and clean, with a starched nurse standing by, smiling prettily. The other showed the same man in the same bed, but the bed hadn't been made for a while and the dressings hadn't been changed and no other attention had been paid to the patient, who was alone and obviously incapable of looking after himself. The flat flash lighting had washed out gradation and detail; nevertheless, it wasn't what you'd call a pretty picture.

I gave the prints back. "If that's the best work Caselius can get done over there," I said, "it's no wonder he had to import a photographer from America."

Wellington said, "One's the kind of picture Taylor gets when she's co-operating nicely. If she balks, she starts getting the other kind. It worked for a while. She went along with Caselius, using her American citizenship and her husband's old contacts and sources for the little man's benefit. Then I guess she sat down and took stock of the situation and decided there was no future in it; and that maybe if she could nail Caselius for us we could do something about getting Hal Taylor back for her. So she came to us with her plan, which you've just finished shooting to hell. Now she's out there somewhere trying to persuade

Caselius that she had nothing to do with it, that I fooled her as much as I did him, so he won't take it out on her husband, wherever he's lying helpless."

"You don't know where they went?" I asked.

He shook his head. "I wanted Grankvist to have them followed, but he wasn't sticking his neck out any further on my sayso. He'd had it, as far as I was concerned."

"You could have followed them yourself," I said. "Instead of coming over here and making with the fists."

He said, "Don't tell me what I could have done, fella. Have you got a drink around here somewhere? All this talking makes me dry."

I said, "You seem to know your way around my suitcase. Find it."

I went to the dresser and got my little plastic cup and my jar of powdered coffee and took them behind the bathroom curtain. I let the water run, waiting for it to turn hot, testing it from time to time with my finger. I thought of Lou Taylor in her tight black pants. I thought of Lou Taylor in her rusty skirt and sweater. I thought of Lou Taylor in her nice black dress, and stopped that line of thought. I heard the big guy in the other room take a couple of swigs out of my plastic flask. Well, the alcohol should kill any germs he might leave, but I still thought I'd wash it off later.

"God, you keep it stuffy in here," I heard him say.

I called back, "If you wouldn't smoke those ropes. . . ."

Then I stopped. He was moving to the window. I could have warned him, I suppose, but he was old enough to vote. He'd been in this business as long as I had. I didn't owe him a thing except a sore jaw and a couple of bruised ribs. To hell with him. I heard the window open. The shot came almost instantly. I walked into the room. There wasn't any hurry. The guy had either missed or he hadn't.

When I came in, Wellington was standing at the open window, his back to me, his hands to his face. I've said they don't have screens, haven't I? There was nothing to stop him when he pitched forward. The last I saw of him was the soles of his shoes. They looked tremendous. He was a big man, all right. It seemed quite a while before he hit the ground, two stories below.

Chapter Twenty-five

As HE'D SAID himself, some guys are tough. When we got to him—Grankvist had left some men on the premises, and being downstairs, they beat me to it—he was breathing and gave promise of continuing to do so for a reasonable length of time, barring further accidents. He was even, after a few minutes, conscious and cursing. The doctor who arrived shortly diagnosed a broken arm, a broken collarbone, an undetermined number of broken ribs, and a neat furrow along the bone above the left eye, caused by a bullet. There seemed to be no serious damage to skull or eye. They took him away to the hospital.

I went back to my room and shaved. I was almost dressed when Grankvist arrived. I let him in, and finished tying my tie, watching him go to the window, look around, and discover for himself where the bullet had buried itself in the wall after glancing off Wellington's cranium.

He said, "You were in there, according to the report I have." He jerked his head toward the curtain.

I nodded. "I didn't shoot him."

"Obviously," Grankvist said. "As a matter of fact, we already have the would-be assassins. Their lorry—truck, I think you call it in America—broke down thirty kilometers east of town. The rifle was still in it. They were caught fleeing into the woods. We haven't yet determined which of the two fired the shot, but it's not a matter of great importance, except perhaps to the court that will try the case." He glanced at me. "You wouldn't want to hazard a guess as to why Herr Wellington should be shot?"

"No," I said, "but he's an hombre who'd naturally have lots of enemies—I mean, of course, because of his business."

Grankvist nodded thoughtfully, and glanced at the window again. "It was still quite dark, was it not? And the light of the room was behind him, and you are both tall

142

men, although he is heavier. And it is your hotel room, not his."

I looked shocked. "Why, son, nobody'd shoot at me!"

"Maybe not," Grankvist said, "but I find it strange how you attract violence and death, Herr Helm. There was a lady in Stockholm, was there not? Had we not thought it essential to our plans that you should be free to proceed to Kiruna with your cameras, you would have been questioned quite thoroughly about that murder, I assure you, although there was some evidence to indicate that you were not responsible. The Stockholm police would like a statement, upon your return. Then there was the man found dead in your hired car, outside this very hotel. Now this unfortunate incident. Somehow I do not think Herr Wellington has been quite frank with me in the matter of your identity. I received a distinct impression of—shall we say?—professional jealousy."

I said without expression, "Naturally, I don't know what you're talking about, Herr Grankvist."

"Naturally," he said. "But please keep in mind, Herr Helm, that we Swedes feel very strongly about violence. We do not even allow our children to watch your American cowboy films. It is our belief that even known criminals and spies are entitled to a fair trial. To simply shoot them down, except in cases of dire necessity, is a travesty of law enforcement. I hope I make myself quite clear." He turned toward the door, and paused. "What is this?"

He'd picked up my flask from the top of my suitcase, where Wellington had left it. "Just a flask with whisky," I said. "It's not illegal, I hope."

"Oh, no," he said. "I was just interested. They make so many interesting things of plastic these days."

As soon as he'd gone I went to the suitcase. I didn't have to look very far; I found it stuck down among my clean, rolled socks, cold and hard to the touch: my little five-shot Smith and Wesson, still fully loaded. I frowned at it for a moment. Grankvist had been cryptic, to say the least. I didn't really know whether he was returning the gun for my protection—after what had happened to Wellington— and warning me sternly not to misuse it, or whether that fancy speech of his had been double-talk to cover up the fact that he was turning me loose with a loaded revolver and his blessing. It's always a little hard to interpret these characters who deal in abstract concepts like law and justice.

I checked the weapon over carefully, since it seemed that the time had come to start wearing it. Then I went over to the hospital to see how my compatriot was getting along. I had a lot of trouble getting through the outer defenses, but finally they let me into Wellington's room. He'd been set and stitched and bandaged by this time. When I closed the door behind me, his eyes opened.

"You sonofabitch," he whispered.

I felt a lot better. Apparently the experience hadn't done a thing for him. He was just going to go right on being the same old objectionable loudmouth. I'd been afraid he might say something to make me feel remorseful.

"You knew they were out there," he whispered.

I moved my shoulders. "It was a possibility," I said. "You should have thought of it. What are you crying about? You're the fellow who was damned if he was going to ask for help from me, remember? Have I got to take you by the hand and lead you around to keep you from targeting yourself at lighted windows?"

We stared at each other for a long moment; then he grinned faintly. "All right," he murmured. "All right, at least you're a consistent bastard. If you'd come in here whining how sorry you were and how you'd have given anything, but anything, to keep me from getting hurt, I'd have spat in your eye." He closed his eyes, and opened them again. "Find my coat, will you?"

It took me a while to track it down, but they finally located it and gave it to me. I took it to the bed.

"Is the door closed?" he whispered.

"It's closed."

"In the lining," he said. "Front right. Use your knife. I guess the damn coat's not worth much any more."

I got out my knife and cut the lining open and found a small spill of paper. I took it back to him.

"Hell, it's gibberish to me," he said irritably. "Don't wave it at me. If it means anything to you, you're welcome to it."

I unrolled the paper and recognized the code. I looked at him, but his eyes were closed again. I took the paper to the table in the corner and worked it out. It had my code number and some transmission signals I didn't recognize since it hadn't come through Vance, who wasn't transmitting messages any more. The station of origin was Washington. The text read:

Original orders operative, changes canceled. Go get him. Mac.

I got out a match and burned the paper. When I went back to the bed, Wellington was wrinkling his nose in distaste.

"You might ask a guy before you stink up his room like that," he whispered.

"Look who's talking," I said.

"Well, are you satisfied? Can you find him?"

"I don't have to find him," I said. "He'll find me. I've got something he wants."

Wellington grimaced under the bandages. "Yeah. I figured that, finally. It just came to me, lying here. You and your goddamn films. You couldn't touch him; you didn't have your orders; I had them. So you let him walk off with a bunch of phonies, fogged so nobody could tell the difference, and kept the real ones to use for bait when the time came."

I said, "I'm listening hard. I seem to recall being accused of doing it for spite. I'm waiting for an apology."

He said, "I ought to sic Grankvist on you again, you human calculating machine."

I looked down at him for a moment longer. Flat on his back, he wasn't such a bad guy. "Anything I can get you?" I asked.

"Yeah," he said. "Caselius. Get the hell out of here. I want to sleep."

When I got back to the hotel, there was a girl talking to the clerk at the desk. This time I recognized the narrow, gaudy pants. Having seen that plaid once, you couldn't forget it. She was still, I saw, wearing her hair pulled smoothly back to the big knot at the neck, like last night. Her profile was wonderful, in the moment before she became aware of me and turned. I thought I'd have to dream up an excuse to photograph her, some time when I had leisure to concentrate on simple things like truth and beauty. At the moment she was just a distraction and a nuisance.

"Good morning, Cousin Elin," I said.

145

"It *was* a good morning," she said. "But it is afternoon now. I was asking for you. I was going for a walk, to take some colored pictures, the leaves are so lovely at this time of year, but my camera is stuck. It will not wind properly. I wondered if you could possibly—"

It was hard to realize that, among some people, life was still going on normally, and pretty girls were still going out to take lousy color slides with which to bore their families and friends in the long winter evenings to come.

"I'll take a look at it," I said. "Come on up to my room. I've got some tools and a changing bag up there."

She gave me the camera as we went up the stairs. It was a little 35mm Zeiss job in that kind of ever-ready case with a flap in front, kind of like the drop seat of grandpa's drawers. When you see a guy packing a case like that, don't bother to ask him what publication he's working for. If he were a pro, he wouldn't be cluttering up his camera with a lot of extraneous leather. I unlocked the door, let her in, followed her inside, closed the door, and went past her to the nearest table.

"I think you've torn the perforations," I said. "That means the sprocket has nothing to engage, so the film won't advance when you wind it. I'll get the changing bag. . . ."

I stopped talking. She'd come up behind me—to look over my shoulder, I thought—but the thing that poked me in the ribs was hard and unmistakable, if totally incredible.

"Don't move!" she said. Her voice was strained. "Don't move or I will shoot. You know what we want. Where is it?"

Chapter Twenty-six

WHERE I trained during the war, they had a subject called preparedness or alertness or some such title. They've toned it down since. I guess it was too rough for peacetime; people sometimes got hurt. When I took my refresher course recently, we just got a couple of inspirational lectures on the subject.

The way it was done in wartime was this: you'd be walking innocently between buildings at the school, or having a beer at the canteen, and you'd be chatting with an off-duty instructor in a friendly manner. Suddenly, smiling, patting you on the back and telling you what a swell guy you were and how he'd never had a pupil like you, he'd produce an unloaded gun and shove it into your side. At least you hoped the gun was unloaded. At that place you were never quite sure. And it wasn't just the instructors; it could be the guy you bunked with, or the pretty girl at the canteen. Your job was to react and react fast, even if it was Mac himself. If you wasted any time in conversation, you flunked the course. . . .

She'd made the usual two mistakes the inexperienced make with a gun: she'd got in too close—why use a gun at all if you're going to work at knife range?—and she'd pointed a gun at a man she wasn't ready to kill. After all, she wanted the films. Dead, I was going to be no use in helping her find them. I won't say I figured this out in detail. You just kind of sense if the climate is favorable, so to speak: have you got a chance or haven't you?

It took me no more time than required to let go of the camera I was holding; then various articles of furniture, one camera, and one pistol, went in various directions. Elin von Hoffman doubled over abruptly, hugging herself where—after striking the gun aside—I'd driven four fingers into her, rigid and together, like the blade of a dagger. I

147

checked myself barely in time to stop the chopping, edge-of-the-hand blow to the neck that was supposed to terminate this particular exercise.

Then I stood there, watching her go to her knees, gagging for breath. I suppose disillusionment is the proper word for what I felt, now that I had time to do some feeling about it. Anger and incredulity were there, too, and a kind of grief. I'd never made a pass at this girl—hadn't even thought of her in those terms—but in some way she'd been a bright and reassuring light in a dark business, something clean and lovely and innocent to remind me that somewhere there was a different kind of world where lived a different kind of people. . . . But obviously there wasn't. It was all the same world, and if you wanted to survive in it, you could damn well keep your guard up. If an angel came down from heaven with a genuine, certified halo, you were still a sucker to turn your back.

I sighed, and set the furniture aright, and picked up and pocketed her gun—one of those little Spanish automatics—and came back to her.

"Get up," I said.

She got up slowly and steadied herself against the table. Presently she smoothed down her gray sweater and reached up to tuck back an escaping wisp of hair. Strangely, she was still beautiful, if a little pale. She rubbed her midsection ruefully, and gave a small laugh.

"That was quite a fine demonstration, Cousin Matthias," she said. "I must say, I did not expect . . . now I really believe you are a dangerous man, as I have been told."

"Thanks," I said. "May I ask how you figure in all this, Cousin Elin?"

"Why," she said calmly, "I am the person who was to get the films from you, perhaps on the train or plane going south. You did not know we were to travel south together, did you? But it would not have been too difficult to arrange, I think. You did not find me unattractive. Or if not then, I would have taken them in Stockholm, or at Torsäter. . . . That was before you suddenly decided to ship them off to America and we had to change our plans."

I was thinking that I should have known. Lou had tried to warn me, for one thing. And then there was the fact that last night, after learning what I planned to do with the films, Lou must have passed the word to somebody. Yet she had not been out of my sight all evening; she'd hardly been out of my hearing, except once at the dinner party when she'd been talking to Elin. . . .

I looked at the girl before me. "Just out of curiosity, is there really such a person as Colonel Stjernhjelm, or did you make him up? And are we really related?"

She laughed. "Colonel Stjernhjelm certainly does exist; he would be indignant to hear that you doubted it. I went to considerable trouble to make his acquaintance. And of course we are related. Sweden is a small country. I do not think there are any of the old families that cannot trace a relationship somewhere." She looked at me and smiled. "You have a reproachful expression, Cousin Matthias. I deceived you, if not in this respect, in others. Well, did you not try to deceive me, too, pretending to be a nice American photographer who didn't know a word of Swedish?" She continued to smile, watching me. *"Vad gör vi nu?"* she asked.

"What do we do now?" I translated. "Why, now we pay a visit to Mister Caselius. *Nu gör vi visit hos Herr Caselius."*

She shook her head gently. "You are much too optimistic. Just because you took my gun away from me. . . . I should not have tried to force you with the gun. It was a mistake. I should have followed my instructions, but I found them distasteful. But one cannot be squeamish in this work, can one, Cousin?"

"I'm interested," I said. "Let's hear more about your instructions."

She said, "I will have to put my hand in my pocket. I am not reaching for a weapon. Please do not hit me again." She didn't wait for a response, but reached down and came up with a small bundle, which she spread on the table. "I think you will recognize these," she said.

I looked. There was a wedding ring, a rather nice engagement diamond, a long cigarette holder, and the large linen handkerchief, no longer quite clean and fresh, that I'd lent to Lou Taylor a few hours ago so that she could dry her eyes. My first feeling was relief. Anyway, she was still alive. At least that was what I was supposed to think.

"Yes," I said. "I recognize them. Where is she?"

"The woman is in our hands. I am to tell you that if the films are not delivered to me, and if I do not appear with them at a certain place within a certain fairly short time,

149

she will die. She will suffer first, and then she will die."

I looked at her, speaking her bloodthirsty lines with a kind of childish innocence. It was obvious that she didn't really know what suffering meant, and if she'd ever seen death, it had been neat and tidy, in a setting of sad organ music and lovely flowers. She was playing an exciting game involving dangerous weapons and melodramatic speeches and, no doubt, pure, rebellious motives of one kind or another. She had a Cause, I was sure. They always do. At that age, they're always saving the world, or some small part of it, from something. I suppose it's a good thing, in a way, even if it makes them suckers for any sharpie with a fast line of talk. Certainly, if the world ever is saved, it'll be by somebody young enough not to know that it can't be done.

As for the threat itself, it was all I could do not to laugh in her face. I mean, they must have been watching TV or something. It was the corny, classic move: grab the heroine and immediately the hero, previously a raging tiger, becomes a little woolly lamb, bleating his concern for his beloved.

I suppose that's okay for the kids who watch those shows. In real life, it doesn't work quite like that. I mean, I'd been sent to do a job, and when you send a man like me to do a job you don't expect him to louse it up any time somebody happens to threaten some stray female he happens to like. Sara Lundgren was dead. She'd had it coming, in a sense; but Vance was dead, too, and he'd been a pretty good man. Others had died, and others were going to die, and if one of them had to be Lou Taylor, it was tough. I'd feel real bad about it, but sentiment is one thing and business is another. I might even have to die myself. I'd feel like hell about that, too.

I started to say something like this, and then I checked myself. After all, it was an opening; it was what I'd been waiting for. Instead, I let my shoulders sag despondently.

"Is she all right?" I asked, looking at the stuff on the table. "He hasn't hurt her, has he?"

"Not yet," Elin said. "Where are the films?"

"What assurance do I have—"

"None," the kid said. "But you do know that if you refuse to co-operate, she will die."

I looked up. "Elin," I said, "you talk big about death,

but have you ever seen anybody dead? Let me tell you about a woman named Sara Lundgren, killed by your friend Caselius with a machine pistol. She took several bullets in the face, and the rest of the burst in the chest. Have you ever seen a pretty woman dead, with part of her jaw shot away and her brains leaking out of the back of her head—"

Elin made a sharp little gesture. "We're wasting time!" Her face was pale. "Where are the films?"

I drew a long breath. "All right," I said resignedly. "All right, but I'm going with you."

It was the right move. It was the thing I was supposed to say. I saw the faint gleam of triumph in her eyes: my reaction was the one she'd been warned to expect, by Caselius, who'd know that in our business we don't have families or lovers or friends. He'd know that no threat to Lou would hold me back—she was a grown woman who had to take her own chances—and he expected me to come, wanted me to come, and was ready for me.

Elin said, with a show of surprise: "Do you expect me to lead you to the man you came here to kill? Do you take me for a fool, Cousin Matthias?"

I hesitated. Then I took her little gun from my pocket and laid it on the table. I hesitated again. Then I took my own gun out from where I was wearing it, tucked under my belt on the left side, butt forward. The agents of the F.B.I., those scientific boys, have determined that the best place to pack a small concealed weapon is on the right hip under the coat, high up, in a holster firmly anchored to the belt. You sweep the coat aside and go for the gun in a single movement. This is fine if you like holsters and are quite sure your right hand is going to be available when the time comes. Personally, I'm opposed to carrying a lot of leather gear—if discovered, it makes you look like a gangster— and if I'm going to break down and wear a firearm, I want it where I can reach it with either hand.

I laid the little Smith and Wesson beside the Spanish pistol. "There's your gun," I said. "And there's mine. Where's the risk? I'm alone. Caselius has at least five men; I met them in Stockholm—"

"No, only two now—" She checked herself quickly, flushing.

I grinned. "Okay. That checks. Two were picked up by the police today, weren't they, after the shooting here at

151

the hotel? Caselius was kind of slow calling them off, wasn't he? If they hadn't shot the wrong man, he'd never have got his films. . . . And then there was the guy last week, shot in the shoulder by my friend Vance. Miracle drugs or no miracle drugs, he'll be out of commission for a while, won't he?"

"He's dead!" Elin said angrily. "Your friend murdered him!"

I said, "I don't think so. Vance said he shot for the shoulder, and he was a boy who could call his shots. If the man's dead, which doesn't grieve me greatly, it's probably because Caselius couldn't be bothered patching up a cripple, and got rid of him. . . . Okay, so he has two men and you, all armed, against one unarmed man. What kind of odds do you people want, anyway?"

She glanced at me and smiled. "Unarmed, Cousin Matthias? What about your little knife? Caselius says you are quite expert in its use."

I sighed, with the air of a man caught trying to pull a fast one. I took the Solingen knife from my pocket and laid it beside the little .38—that damn little revolver that we'd gone to so much trouble to get into the country. Well, that was the way it went. You spent weeks providing yourself with arms and explosives, and laid elaborate plans for their use, and then half the time you wound up doing the job barehanded. It was like my pretending not to know Swedish, another waste of time. I might have learned something important that way, but as it turned out, I hadn't.

"All right," Elin said slowly. "All right, I will take you. Now give me the films."

I went to the closet and pulled out the metal cartridge boxes, painted white to reflect the hot sun of my native state. Suddenly I found myself very homesick for the sight of a nice red sandstone butte, or a cute little gila monster. I flipped the lids up, displaying the solid masses of film inside.

"There you are," I said. "You'll find what you want down near the bottom. Take every box with a pencil dot in the 'a' of Kodak. No sense in my helping you, since you'd insist on checking my work anyway. I'll see if I can find you a couple of paper bags and some strong string."

Chapter Twenty-seven

LEAVING the hotel with her, I couldn't help being aware that I stood a good chance of running into an ambush anywhere along the line. Chance was too mild a word: it was a certainty that Caselius had something nice all figured out for me. Having used me, he'd want to get rid of me now, so he could relax and stop looking over his shoulder. It could be something very simple. There was even a possibility—Caselius' accomplices being strictly expendable, as Sara Lundgren had found out—that there would be somebody stationed outside the hotel to mow us both down, grab the packages of film, and run.

We made it without incident, however, and then we walked some distance, which didn't help the state of my nerves. When we reached the car, it looked familiar, which could explain why she'd parked it so far away. It was the same taillight-heavy Ford that Caselius—Raoul Carlsson then—had been driving the night he'd almost run me off the road in my little rented Volvo. Elin took the wheel. The sight of her expertly handling Caselius' car seemed to bring home what I'd learned about her. It made her a complete stranger, someone I'd have to learn to know all over again, if I decided it was worth the trouble and if I lived that long.

As we left Kiruna behind, she said, "These big American cars are terrible. So soft, like perambulators swaying on their springs. And these automatic gears—you Americans must not like to drive, or you would not invent such intricate machinery to do the driving for you."

If she was trying to pick an argument, she'd come to the wrong man. You couldn't give me an automatic transmission if you threw a Cadillac in with the deal. I've done some racing and I enjoy shifting gears. But it was hardly the time to discuss the shortcomings of Detroit iron.

"That's right," I said. "I remember. You're the Jaguar-and-Lambretta kid." I watched the wilderness going past the window. "Where are we going?"

She gave me a secretive smile. "I will tell you only this much: it is a cabin on a lake upon which a small airplane with floats will land when the proper signal is sent." She glanced at me, and added slyly, "I am afraid you are going to have to walk a considerable distance, but I will try to pick the easiest way."

Proudly masculine, I started to tell this cocky girl that I could damn well go anywhere she could, but I shut up quickly. If she wanted to consider me helpless in the woods, why should I disillusion her? Upon reflection, it seemed like a notion that deserved encouragement. . . .

We drove eastward at a fast clip. The highway was gravel, but wide and well-graded, the nice, friendly, informal kind of road we used to have out west before they went crazy and started pouring asphalt on every little track across the desert. Around us, the arctic foliage still retained its bright fall colors. There was a low bush with small red leaves that grew everywhere, so that the ground seemed to be on fire. Presently Elin turned into a small logging road heading off in a northerly direction. It turned into a couple of ruts, and then into a trail full of mud holes. She stopped the car and got out.

"From here we must walk," she said.

"How far is it?" I asked, showing no enthusiasm for the prospect.

"About one Swedish mile: ten kilometers. That is about six of your English miles."

I said, "Six and a quarter, to be more precise, one English mile being equal to one and six-tenths kilometers."

She flushed slightly. "I am sorry. I do keep trying to educate you, don't I?"

I looked at her for a moment. The trouble with people is that they're practically all human. It would be much easier if they weren't. This kid had shoved a gun in my back, and threatened Lou with torture and death, but I couldn't seem to hate her very hard. As a matter of fact, I still kind of liked her, I discovered. I won't say her being lovely didn't influence me a little.

"Let's go," I said shortly. "The damn trail won't get any shorter from our standing here looking at it."

She said abruptly, "They will kill you, Matt."

"It's been tried," I said. "So far, unsuccessfully."

"But—" She checked herself, hesitated, swung around, and started into the forest with that businesslike foot-traveler's stride I'd seen before. Following behind, I said, "Caselius must value his privacy highly, to hike six miles every time he wants to reach his headquarters."

"It is only a rendezvous," she said without looking around. "It was only intended as a place to meet once. A place to leave from. A place for the airplane to come, where it could not be seen or heard."

"So he's leaving the country."

"Yes." Still without turning her head, Elin said, "You must love her very much, to deliberately walk into danger for her."

"It's not that," I said. "I just feel kind of responsible for putting her on the spot. If it hadn't been for my trick with the films, Caselius would be in jail and she'd be safe." After a moment I added, "Lou's all right. I won't say I'm not fond of her, but I don't make a habit of wasting undying passion on married women. She's still got a husband around somewhere."

The girl ahead of me didn't actually break step, but her foot kind of hesitated in midair before she put it down. "Has she?"

"What do you mean?" I asked innocently. "Isn't that how Caselius has been keeping her in line, by holding her husband prisoner?"

"She is a fool," Elin said scornfully. "Her husband died of his injuries six months ago. Caselius has been fooling her ever since. One heavily bandaged man in a hospital bed looks very much like another, if the photograph is bad enough. . . ." She threw a quick, suspicious glance over her shoulder. "You knew?"

"I guessed, when I saw the pix," I said. "After all, I really am a photographer of sorts, you know. I couldn't help wondering why he'd have such lousy shots taken when he'd be bound to have somebody around who could take good ones."

I heard her laugh, striding ahead of me briskly. "You are quite clever. . . . Am I walking too fast for you?"

I said, breathing heavily, "Well, we're not standing still, that's for sure."

155

"I will go slower," she said. "It is too bad we cannot drive you in that fine American car with its soft springs and its wonderful automatic transmission." She laughed again. "How can you believe America is going to win, Cousin? How can one conquer the world sitting down?"

After that, we didn't have much breath for conversation. The kid was a walking fool, and despite her promise to slow down she continued to set a killing pace. The country was the wettest I'd ever hiked through. Although I hadn't noticed an abnormal amount of rain during the week I'd been there, the ground seemed to be saturated almost everywhere. We jumped little creeks, splashed through puddles, and waded through boggy hollows. Our shoes were soaked after the first quarter mile. I suppose the solid granite of the earth's core is so close to the surface up here—the soil is so thin—that any rain that falls has no place to go.

Finally I called a rest and sat down on a boulder, panting. She didn't deign to admit weariness; kids never do. She just stood there waiting. Aside from wet feet, the only sign of distress she showed—if you could call it that—was the fact that her soft, light-brown hair, loosened by her exertions and snagged by branches along the way, was falling untidily out of its neat, pulled-back arrangement. Presently she reached up, removed a few pins and a contraption that seemed to be made of horsehair, and shook it all lose about her shoulders.

"Elin," I said. "Tell me. What are you getting out of all this?"

She threw me a quick glance. Her voice was stiff when she spoke. "I am not ashamed."

"Fine," I said. "You're not ashamed. I'll make a note for the record: Elin von Hoffman is not ashamed."

She said, "You would not understand. You are an American, not a Swede. America must be a wonderful country in which to live. At least for the moment, you are both free and powerful. And you have no history to remember and regret."

"Now, listen—"

She made an impatient gesture. "American history is a joke! Why, Columbus did not discover the New World until almost the year fifteen hundred. We have churches still in use here in Sweden dating from twelve hundred, and all they indicate is the time of the arrival of Christianity.

156

Much Swedish history, as you must recall, was made earlier by men who worshiped Odin and Thor. By the time your American history was fairly begun, Swedish history was almost ended."

"I'm slow," I said. "You're leading up to something, but I haven't got it yet."

"Now America is a great power," she said, "and Sweden is a little neutral country, cowering between two giants she must not antagonize on any account. We must be careful, we are told, we must be prudent. . . . Bah! Can we forget that there was a time when the dragon ships would put to sea each spring, and the crews would cast lots to see whether they would take their tribute, this year, from east or from west? And all along the coast of Europe, people trembled awaiting their coming!"

"What are you suggesting," I asked, "that we gather together a bunch of congenial Vikings and go a-raiding?"

She gave me an indignant look. "You joke," she said, "but it is no joke! Once Norway was ours, and Finland and Denmark; the Baltic was a Swedish lake. When Swedish armies moved, the world held its breath, waiting to see where they would strike. We had real kings in those days, not just a family of handsome figureheads imported from France, whose function is to make palatable these little socialists and their comfortable welfare state!" She drew a long breath. "If we are to have royalty, let's have royalty that rules—and fights! Or let us get rid of the whole cowardly pack of princes and politicians and get a government that will recognize that these are days of decision for the whole world. Sweden cannot hide from what is to come under a word called neutrality, like a cur dog hiding under a broken basket. We must take a stand. We must make our choice!"

I said, "It's pretty clear what choice you've made."

"Somebody will rule the world, Matthew Helm! Will it be the country that spends its time and ingenuity saving its people from the dreadful effort of shifting gears? You Americans have almost forgotten how to walk; how can you fight? I do not like these Slavs with their silly political theories, but they have the strength and they have the will, and one cannot be sentimental in these matters. And when it is all over, what country will they select to form the nucleus of the great Scandinavian state that must come?

157

Will it be Finland, that fought them savagely and hates them bitterly? Will it be Norway, that joined your North Atlantic pact against them? Will it be Denmark, geographically and politically aligned with the continent, rather than with us here in the north?" She moved her shoulders abruptly. "It is not what one would choose for one's country, perhaps, but who is free to choose? And who knows, if the giants kill or weaken each other, maybe the time of the pygmies will come!"

I said, "Elin, I'm no world strategist, but I know that for years—centuries—the Russians have been trying to break through to a warm-water port on the Atlantic. It's even more important these days, when the nuclear submarine may become one of the deciding factors of world power. They've got access to the Pacific, but they're still hemmed in on this side of the world. The Black Sea can be blocked at the Dardanelles. The Baltic can be closed almost as easily. Murmansk, way up there on the Arctic Ocean, is a hell of a place to get into and out of, as our boys learned during the war.

"Narvik, in Norway, could be the answer. But you can't reach Narvik by land except through north Sweden, not from the direction of Russia, anyway. I don't say it will happen this year, or the next, but they're considering it, or they wouldn't go to all this trouble to get pictures of the area." I gestured toward the two paper-wrapped packages she carried. "And you're helping them."

She shrugged her shoulders again, under the gray ski sweater. "Nothing is free," she said. "If one wants powerful allies, one must pay a price. What we lose now we may be able to take back later, when they are weakened by war."

She was a real little old Machiavelli, in her fouled-up way. I couldn't tell how much of this she really believed, and how much was a rationalization of the fact that the world was going to hell in a basket and she simply had to do *something* about it, even if what she did was the wrong thing. Some people just aren't built to sit around on their butts being carefully neutral.

She broke off the argument by turning away and starting off again fast. I set off after her. She was half running. I contented myself with following at a jog trot. Gradually, as she slowed after the first spurt, I gained on her. When she heard me coming, she increased her pace again, keeping well ahead of me. I'd catch glimpses of her through the trees, moving rapidly. I'd lose her for several minutes and then see her far ahead, waiting for me, and her laughter would come back to me, mocking me, as she set off again.

When she let me catch her at last, she was sitting on a log at the edge of a great open space that looked at first glance like a wilderness meadow. She looked at me as I slumped down beside her, gasping for breath; and she laughed.

"You do not keep up very well, Cousin Matthias."

"I'm here," I panted.

She waved her hand at the meadow before us. "It looks harmless, does it not, like a pasture for cows. It is a *myr*. The word is the same, I think, as the English 'moor', or maybe 'mire'. In spring it is a bottomless bog and quite impassable; reindeer that venture out upon it disappear from sight and are never seen again. Now in the autumn the ground is not quite so wet, and it can be crossed if one knows how. But one must be careful." She glanced at me again, and said, "Listen."

I frowned. "Listen to what?"

She shook her head sharply. "Be quiet. Just listen!"

I listened. After a moment, I got what she meant. There wasn't anything to hear. In all that flaming country, red and gold to the horizon, not an insect buzzed, not a bird sang. The sky was blue and clear. A breath of air rustled a few dry leaves nearby. Otherwise not a sound broke the great northern silence.

Elin glanced at me. "In our Swedish schools we have a course called 'orientation'. Every Swedish child must learn how to find his way across unknown country without getting lost. Do you have such classes in America?"

"No," I said.

She asked gently, "Do you know where we are, Cousin Matthias?"

"No," I said, honestly enough. I knew which direction the highway was, which is as much as you generally knew, hiking through the bush. But that wasn't the question she'd asked.

She rose and stood looking down at me for a moment. "Go back," she said. "Walk due south. You will strike the road after a while. Go that way." She pointed. It was the right direction. She said, "If you come with me, they will kill you. They are waiting for you, armed. I am supposed to lead you up to their guns. But I cannot do it. After all, we are related, even if very distantly. Go back."

I hesitated, and shook my head. She looked at me for a moment longer and started to say something else; then she laughed instead.

"You are stubborn," she said. "I will not argue with you. The *myr* has better arguments than I have. Just remember the direction to the highway. This is a nice country in which to be lost."

She turned and headed out across that innocent-looking meadow. I followed her. Soon we were jumping from one grassy hummock to the next. Between them the mud was soft and black. This was easy. Then we came to a small stream, bordered by a low but almost impassable tangle of what looked like mountain laurel. You couldn't break a path through the stuff, you had to do a kind of dance on top of it, putting your feet where the twisted roots and branches looked as if they would bear your weight. If you misjudged, you went through into the mud beneath and had to fight your way back up to the top again.

The stream itself was crystal clear, too wide for jumping and too deep for comfort, and icy cold. After that we had laurel again, and finally we struggled up on dry ground that didn't last very long. It was only a little piny island in the middle of the bog. Beyond it, after a few more grassy hummocks, was just plain mud, black and shiny.

The area was only some fifty yards wide, but it stretched a much greater distance in either direction. There was no way of getting around it that I could see. On the other side, invitingly near beyond a stretch of marsh grass, was the edge of the forest. But first there was the muck to get across.

I glanced at Elin. She wasn't a movie heroine; she hadn't come through the ordeal totally unscathed. But then, she hadn't even been a spit-and-polish girl. That lousy blue dress in which I'd first seen her had been less becoming than her present splashed and muddy outfit. At least now she'd licked and bitten off that nauseating lipstick she liked to wear. Flushed and bright-eyed with exercise, she looked kind of breathtaking, as a matter of fact.

I jerked my head toward the black stuff. "You're the guide," I said. "How do we get around that?"

"Get around?" she said, smiling. "What is the matter,

160

Cousin Matthias, are you afraid?"

She walked directly out there. After two steps she was going in almost to her knees, and the whole great expanse was rippling and wobbling like a bowl of jello. She threw a glance over her shoulder.

"It is all right," she said. "It is all right, if you keep moving. Of course, if you stop, you will sink very quickly."

I said sharply, "Come back here!"

She kept on wading, clutching the packages of film. I suppose she should have looked ridiculous. A beautiful girl has no business performing acts of strength and courage; our civilization isn't geared for it. Women aren't supposed to do anything that'll muss their hair or endanger their nylons; and wading through knee-deep mud isn't exactly a glamorous occupation. Just the same, the kid had guts. I really didn't like the looks of that stuff at all.

"Come back, you crazy little fool!" I shouted.

I started after her, and retreated quickly. I heard her laugh, and she kept on going. On the other shore she paused to fix a muddy shoestring that apparently had come untied. Then, wiping her hands on the seat of her pants, she straightened up and looked at me across the lake of mud. She pointed to the south, the direction of the highway, the direction I was supposed to go. Then she picked up the packages of film and disappeared into the woods.

Chapter Twenty-eight

AFTER A LITTLE, I glanced at my watch to note the time. It seemed likely that she'd sneak back to see what I'd do next, to make sure she'd really lost me. I therefore made a show of trying to find a safe way around that overgrown muck hole. I circled far to the right, as far as the grasss and hummocks would take me, but there was no solid path across the stuff. I returned to the island, waded out once more the way she'd gone, and retreated with a display of panic after going in to my knees. I made a swing to the left and had no luck there, either. Finally I went back to the island again and stood looking glumly at the spot on the shoreline where she'd disappeared. I restrained myself from shaking my fist at it. You've got to use moderation in these things.

Having put on enough of a performance, I figured, to deceive several tall, beautiful, overconfident young ladies in plaid pants, I turned dejectedly and shuffled back the way we'd come. As soon as I was out of sight, I lay down under a pine tree, put my hat over my eyes, and concentrated on resting up for the next phase of the operation. I tried not to think of anything, not even Lou and the danger she was in. It wasn't something I could allow to affect my actions. There wasn't anything else to think about. The final hand had been dealt. All that was left was to play the cards.

I gave her half an hour by the watch. If she'd been older, or more experienced, or less cockily sure of my general uselessness, I'd have made it an hour; but I was betting she couldn't stay still nearly that long, watching an empty patch of swamp. When the time was up, I rose, put my hat firmly on my head, and waded across the mud flat, following her footsteps, already filling and fading from sight. It wasn't nice stuff at all. I don't know as I'd have tried it, coming on it cold. You kind of expected the whole nasty quivering black mass to split open and swallow you. But what the hell, I had big feet to support me, and if she could do it, I could.

On the other side, I spent a little time remembering my woodcraft and untangling her tracks. As I'd suspected, she'd gone only a short way before returning to watch my antics. I found the place where she'd lain in the shoreline brush, spying on me. Her elbow marks, in the soft ground, even showed the weave of her sweater.

Then she'd got up and started out again; and now, as I'd hoped and planned, having got rid of me, she'd stopped fooling around. We'd come pretty far north while playing tag through the brush, but now her trail ran considerably south of east, angling back toward the highway. Well, I'd never taken much stock in that hideaway six miles back in the boondocks. Lovely Elin was a cross-country type, to be sure, but the little man, Caselius, wasn't. After all, I'd checked him out once, on a dark road, sword in hand; he'd started out strong but he'd faded fast. Even a two-mile hike along a cleared trail would be a hardship for that little fashion plate. He was a lad who worked with his brain and left the muscle to others, except occasionally when there was an interesting spot of shooting to be done. It doesn't take much strength or endurance to pull a trigger.

The sign on the ground said Elin had written me off. She was making no effort at concealment; it simply didn't occur to her that she might be tracked. I could follow the trail at a steady lope. I found it a lot easier to maintain the pace, now that I no longer had to pretend to be on the verge of collapsing from exhaustion. For a while there, puffing and panting, I'd almost had myself fooled.

What the kid hadn't counted on, apparently, was that we've got a few wilderness areas on our side of the water, too. This myth of the soft and helpless American is soothing to European egos, and may even contain a grain of truth, but there are still a few of us left who know the big woods, and the big deserts, too. And while thirty-six might seem ancient by her standards, it wasn't quite senile; and I'd just had a course of training that had put me in pretty good condition, even if my instructors hadn't been greatly impressed. I had another advantage that hadn't occurred to her. I'd spent most of my postwar life exercising my lungs on the thin air of my home in Santa Fe, at an altitude higher than the highest peak in Scandinavia; I had lung-power to burn. And while I'm no proponent of the double standard in other respects, I think the athletic records will bear me out when I say a good man can run down a good woman any day in the week—and if you want to build that into a dirty joke, bud, you just go right ahead.

I won't say it was fun, loping through the arctic forest at that easy jog trot that eats up the miles. Her tracks said she wasn't straining herself a bit to keep ahead of me, never suspecting there was anybody to keep ahead of. She was just walking along at a good clip, making an occasional detour to avoid the bad spots but swinging right back to her line as soon as the going was easy again. She knew her stuff all right, whether she'd learned it in school or elsewhere. It was that kind of rolling country without prominent landmarks in which regiments of hunters get hopelessly lost each year, but her trail never faltered. . . . It wasn't fun, exactly. For one thing, it was work, and I don't like exercise any more than the next guy. For another, it seemed likely that I'd have some dirty business coming up before the day was over. Still, after all the play-acting and horsing around, it was nice to be out in the open on a fine day with the end in sight.

Presently I spotted the bright plaid pants ahead of me —not as bright as they had been earlier in the day, but still a strong alien pattern in the light and shade of the forest. She was moving more slowly now, beginning to tire a little. Every now and then she'd sit down and rest. I had it harder now. I had to move quietly so she wouldn't hear me, and I had to be careful not to overrun her when she stopped. By the time she reached the road she was looking for, I was pretty tired myself.

It was an old, overgrown logging road running approximately north and south. Like any good woodsman, she'd given herself some leeway. Walking across unknown, trailless country, you can't be sure of striking a given point, like a camp or cabin; I don't care if you're Dan'l Boone himself. You *can* be fairly certain of intercepting a line of reasonable length, however, like the road leading to said camp or cabin. So you keep well to the safe side until you strike your road, and then follow it home.

She turned north again. I had it really rough, now. She was striding easily along an open trail, not clear enough

164

for vehicles, to be sure, but a paved highway for a walker. I was out in the woods traveling parallel to her course trying to be quiet as I fought my way through brush and over fallen timber. I didn't know who'd be waiting along that road, and I didn't want my tracks on it in case they had somebody wandering around who could read sign.

The precaution paid off sooner than I'd expected. She went around a bend and up the long straight stretch that followed; she'd almost reached the next turn when somebody whistled softly, calling her back. He'd let her get far enough ahead to make sure she wasn't followed, before announcing himself.

She turned and came back. The man stepped out into the road. His face was vaguely familiar; I thought I'd met him before, or his fist, in the park in Stockholm. Sara Lundgren would probably have recognized him, too. He had a brief conversation with Elin. I couldn't hear what they were saying, but presently he whistled again, and another man stepped out into the road from the other side. They'd had that long straight stretch covered, ready to cut down anybody who started down it. If I'd come walking along there with Elin, I suspect we'd both have died. Both men were packing automatic weapons, which are notoriously unselective, and it seemed unlikely they'd have risked losing me just to give her time to reach cover.

I felt a funny sense of responsibility, looking at that beautiful screwball kid standing there in her muddy pants and her snagged sweater. She was literally just a babe in the woods. She might talk big about dirty work on the international level, but it had obviously never occurred to her that a man might deliberately use her and shoot her down, any more than it had occurred to Sara Lundgren. I watched one of the men take the packets of film from her. He spoke to her, and started off along the road, and she went with him. The other man watched them go, then stepped back into his hiding place in the bushes.

I suppose I could have left him there, but I needed his weapon; and I don't like leaving men behind me, anyway, when it can be helped. It was an easy stalk. He wasn't expecting trouble. At the last moment, a twig snapped under my foot and he swung around sharply, just in time to catch the blow to the throat that crushes the windpipe. My instructors at the training school would have been proud of me. He never got to make a sound. I even managed to catch his machine pistol before it hit the ground—not that it mattered greatly, since he never got the safety off.

It was a make of gun I'd had no experience with, but the various buttons and levers were self-explanatory: there was the safety, the trigger, and a selector switch to change the piece from full- to semi-automatic. Everybody's gone hog-wild over these ugly little squirt guns lately, and I can never quite see why, except that nobody seems to want to take the trouble to really learn to shoot, so they've got to have weapons they can spray like a hose. Personally, I prefer a scope-sighted rifle for long range; and for close-up work a short-barreled pump or automatic shotgun loaded with buckshot makes a lovely weapon. However, you can't always satisfy your preferences. I had a machine pistol. It would have to do.

I set the thing to fire single shots. The dead man in the bushes was already concealed from the road. I left him lying there and hurried after Elin and her escort. Soon I came to the edge of an open, logged-over space with the stumps still standing, turning gray with age. There was a small lake, little more than a forest pond, and a cabin, little more than a tarpaper shack, with a rusty stove-pipe jutting from the roof at a precarious angle. The place had a deserted air. It looked as if it had stood empty for years, sheltering nothing but mice and pack rats, if they had pack rats in this country.

Elin was walking with her companion across the clearing away from me, toward the cabin. She'd obviously had it. Keeping up with the man's long stride was clearly an effort for her. Well, she'd given me quite a run.

I couldn't help thinking, as I watched her, that a girl like this might be kind of nice to have around. She'd out-grow her crackpot political ideas soon enough; and with her looks, who cared about her taste in clothes? I mean, women who can cook and make love are a dime a dozen, but a kid who can strike out across rough country on her own, and hit her destination like a homing pigeon—that's something pretty special. There is a lake up in the Sangre de Cristos where the trout grow to fifteen inches and the deer all come with heads like hatracks. There is a place in the San Luis Valley where the ducks come in with the dawn. . . .

166

I woke up; it was no time for daydreaming. I had business to attend to. I found a place to lie near the base of a tree, where a fallen log gave me a rest for the gun. I settled myself comfortably, and swung the sights across Elin and the man to the cabin door. I held that sight picture for almost a minute, hoping Caselius would make my job easy by coming out to meet them—after all, my primary business was with him. But he didn't show, and they were getting close, and I couldn't afford to let reinforcements into the place. I swung the piece back to cover the man beside Elin, and pressed the trigger gently.

The squirt gun didn't have much in the way of noise and recoil. It didn't have much punch, either, at that range. I saw my man jerk, and knew I'd got a solid hit somewhere in the thorax area, but that lousy little jacketed bullet didn't knock him down or even stagger him badly. He started to turn, swinging his own weapon toward me. I fired again. He went to his knees, still trying stubbornly to get lined up to shoot back. It took a third bullet to put him down. God damn those lousy little pipsqueak weapons, anyway. Most states back home would call them illegal for deer, but I guess these armaments specialists figure it doesn't much matter what you shoot a man with.

My heart was acting up a little now. The dance was open and the music was playing. I swung back to cover the cabin door, saw nobody there, and looked at Elin von Hoffman. The kid was bending over the fallen man. She raised her head to look in my direction. I thought I could see an incredulous look on her lovely, dirty face, even at that distance. There may even have been something of reproach: after all, she'd given me a break, out there in the woods.

She stared at me, or at the spot from which my shots had come, for several seconds. Then she snatched up the fallen machine pistol and ran for the cabin door, just as a blunt automatic poked out there and spat noise and flame. . . .

I don't suppose we'll ever know his precise motives. Maybe he thought she'd betrayed him. Maybe he thought she was attacking him, with that businesslike weapon in her hands. Maybe he was shooting at me—although the range was long for a hand gun—and she just ran into the line of fire. My own theory is that he was merely wiping her out angrily because she'd been inefficient. She'd brought trouble to Caselius; she deserved to die; and he was just the boy to see that she got her deserts.

I could see nothing to shoot at, but I put a bullet through that doorjamb on his side, hoping. Like most hope shots, it was a dud. It was too late, anyway. She was lying there in the sunshine, a small crumpled heap. Beside her lay the machine pistol. Behind her, near the dead man, lay the two packets of film she'd brought such a long distance. I could have felt bad about that, too, if I'd let myself. Well, she'd never know she'd wasted all that effort on blank film. I'd gone over the marked boxes with artgum that morning, and marked up another batch for purposes of bait. I won't say I felt any particular obligation to Grankvist or his government; but it always helps to keep an ace in the hole, and I had lots of film. Even if Caselius should get me, I'd still have the last laugh when his technicians pulled the stuff out of the soup and he discovered he'd fallen for the same gag twice.

There was silence for a while, after all the noise, but the little man inside made his decision fast. He didn't sit around hoping for help from his guard up the road. He gave me credit, at last, for brains and ruthlessness equal to his own; I wouldn't be out front shooting off firearms loudly if I hadn't already cleaned up the premises. And the day wasn't getting any younger, and I guess waiting for darkness didn't appeal to him. He wasn't a wilderness boy himself, and I'd just proved I was. He had reason to know I could handle a knife, and he wasn't aware I had no blade with me. And there are a lot of otherwise brave men who prefer not to wait for a knifeman in the dark.

He decided to take his chances with the gun, while daylight lasted, and he made the obvious play. The door opened and Lou came out. She looked pretty good at a distance. I could tell that she hadn't been drastically abused, at any rate. She seemed to be kind of dusty, that was all—not surprising, considering the place where she'd been kept. She came out, still wearing her black beatnik outfit, with her hands tied behind her. Caselius, followed, no taller than she, holding his pistol in her back. He was pretty dusty too, and his hair needed combing. It was longer than you'd have expected, meeting him normally; and, disheveled, it gave him a wild look.

Pausing beside the dead girl, he snatched up the weapon

she'd dropped, tucking his pistol inside his belt. This put us on even terms, with maybe a slight balance in his favor, since it was a weapon he knew and liked, and he also had Lou. They kept on coming until they reached the dead man on the ground. Caselius spoke a command, and Lou picked up the packages of film. He crouched down behind her as she did so, not exposing himself a bit. They went on past the dead man and a little farther. Caselius gave another order, and Lou stopped, with the muzzle of the gun in her back.

Caselius raised his voice. "Helm. Helm, are you there?"

I called back, "I'm here."

He shouted, "Throw out your gun and come in sight with your hands up. You have ten seconds before I shoot Mrs. Taylor to death. One, two. . . ."

I let him hear me laugh. He was running that gag into the ground. He must really have been watching American TV, the corny ideas he kept kicking around.

"Go ahead, little man," I shouted. "When you shoot, she falls. When she falls, you're standing there naked. I've got the sights right in line. I'm waiting."

He stood there a moment longer. He didn't resume his count. Presently he spoke to Lou, and they started moving again. As they came closer, he swung her to one side to keep her between us as they passed my position. My problem was simple enough. I merely had to shoot him. Even if I had to reach him through Lou's body, it was better than letting them get away together. Wounded, she still had a chance of living—she'd already survived one bullet from a weapon similar to the gun I held. If he once got clear, however, and no longer needed her as a shield, she'd certainly die. . . .

But I decided to try less drastic measures first. I stood up in plain sight, to tease him. He'd closed the range enough now so that it was an easy shot for both of us. But of course he was protected by Lou, while I was protected by the fact that his weapon was pressed against Lou's back.

I saw him fight it out with himself and lose. He was thinking, of course, of the long, impossible walk along that brushy road with me hovering nearby, maneuvering for one clear, safe shot. If he could only get rid of me now. . . . Suddenly he snatched the gun out of her back and swung it toward me one-handed, holding her before him with an

169

arm across her throat. The chopper began to speak, but it was a heavy weapon for a little man to work with one hand. His aim was off. The bullets sprayed dirt to my left, and for the moment Lou was not threatened.

I lowered my aim slightly. I had four legs to choose from. She could have made it easier for me by sticking to skirts, but I got what I hoped was a male pants-leg, steadied down on it, and fired.

He slumped down, carrying her with him. His gun ceased firing. Then, to my relief, Lou was free and running, and I had him at last. He knew it, of course. He knew that the sights were in line and that my finger was bearing hard on the trigger. He made the last play in the book. Kneeling there, he flung the machine pistol violently aside. He snatched the automatic from his belt and threw that away. He stuck his arms high in the air.

"I surrender!" he shouted. "See, I am unarmed! I surren—"

Like I say, he must have been watching TV. Or reading books about sentimental Americans. I shoved the selector to full automatic. The burst cut him short and knocked him down.

Then I stood there for a minute or so, watching him. It's not advisable to walk up on them too soon. But he didn't move, lying there, and I went up and turned him over and saw he was quite dead. Lou had had sense enough to throw herself flat after getting clear. Now, with her hands tied behind her, she was having trouble rising. I went over and helped her up. I had nothing with which to cut the ropes, and she'd pulled the knots pretty tight. It took a little time for me to pick them open.

"All right?" I asked.

"Yes," she said. "Yes, I'm all right."

In real life, somehow, you don't embrace the girl and settle the details of your future together while smoke still trickles from the barrel of your gun and the body of your adversary lies warm on the ground before you. I left her there, rubbing her wrists, and went back to the cabin. Halfway there, I started to run. The smaller of the two figures on the ground had changed position since I'd seen it last.

Elin's eyes were open when I came hurrying up to kneel beside her, but I couldn't be sure they were seeing me until her lips moved.

"You . . . tricked me, Cousin Matthias."

I had to clear my throat. "You shouldn't ever give a man like that a break, kid. Or any man, when the chips are down."

"A break?" she whispered. "The chips?" The Americanisms confused her. She frowned. "I wish. . . ." she said. "I wish. . . ."

I never did learn what she wished—maybe to keep on living. Her voice just stopped. Her eyes remained open, until I closed them. I found a blanket in the cabin to spread over her.

Lou had already started down the logging track toward the highway. When I caught up with her, she was standing quite still, looking at the dead man I'd left in the bushes at the side of the road. His head was at a peculiar angle to his body. Her face was very pale. She glanced at me and started walking again. I fell in step beside her. We didn't talk, all the way back to civilization. There wasn't anything to say that wouldn't keep till later.

Chapter Twenty-nine

IN KIRUNA, we got snarled up in a running mile of red tape. When I finally had time and liberty to look for Lou, she was gone. Inquiry disclosed that, having answered all the questions and signed all the papers required of her, she'd grabbed the next plane south. I suppose I could have learned her destination, being a trained undercover man, but I didn't make the effort. If she'd wanted me to know, she'd have left a message for me. If she wanted to see me again, she knew I'd be in Stockholm presently. I wouldn't be hard to find.

I went hunting, instead. Somehow, after all the talk about Colonel Stjernhjelm and the family estate at Torsäter, I felt obliged to go there and talk to the old gentleman. He was very pleasant. I never did discover how much of the story he knew—probably all of it. After all, he had a military title, and Sweden is a small country.

My hunting luck was in. On the second day a bull moose with a fine head wandered past my stand. I had a real gun in my hands, no little pipsqueak squirt gun, but somehow I never got around to pulling the trigger. I just watched the big beast saunter out of sight. He'd never done anything to me, and I wasn't under orders. Like most sentimental gestures, it didn't accomplish a thing. The fellow in the next stand knocked him over with a 9mm Mauser. The next day I was in Stockholm, where more red tape of various kinds awaited me.

Somehow, a couple of weeks got away from me there before, on a hunch, I wandered one evening into the restaurant to which I'd taken Lou the first day I'd met her. A good Stockholm restaurant, even one with music and dancing, is never noisy. I don't know how they manage it, but a roomful of Swedes can do their eating, drinking, talking, and laughing at a sound level several decibels lower than that of the same number of Americans. I don't say this as a

172

reflection upon my native land. It's merely an observation of fact.

Sitting alone at a table for two by the wall, not really expecting much of anything to happen, I found it quiet enough to reread, with complete concentration, a letter I'd just received. So when someone spoke my name, I was startled. I recognized the strange, husky voice at once, of course. It wasn't a voice you forgot. I scrambled to my feet. She was standing there with the headwaiter who, on seeing that she was taken care of, bowed and retired.

"Hello, Matt," she said.

"Hi, Lou."

She hadn't changed much. She was still wearing her hair quite short. Well, it hadn't really had time to grow much. She had a new dress on, navy blue, with a full skirt and a kind of stiff, stand-up collar. It looked like the simple kind of button-up-the-front dress a girl might wear to work, done in a more glamorous material. The dress and supporting petticoats rustled nicely when she sat down. I sat down. We looked at each other for a while in silence.

Abruptly she said, "I just had to think things out, Matt. I had to get used to the idea that Hal was really dead."

"You didn't know?" I said.

"I . . . I wasn't quite sure," she said. "I suspected it, of course, or I'd never have risked approaching an American agent, but there were times. . . . Like after Caselius was arrested and everything started going wrong. Suddenly I was quite sure Hal was alive and I'd gambled with his life and lost. Of course, I never told anybody, not even Wellington, that I thought Hal might be dead. If there had been a leak, if it had got to Caselius, he'd have known I was double-crossing him." This was ancient history. She made a gesture of dismissing it. "What's the letter, if I'm not prying?"

"From my wife," I said. "My ex-wife, I should say. It's now official, and she's met a wonderful man, a rancher, who just loves the kids. They love him, too. Or maybe they love his horses. The boys, at least, were always nuts about riding. I'm not to worry about the support money specified in the decree. Whenever I can pay it is all right, and she'll put it in a fund for their college educations. She didn't ask any alimony, you know. She's well and hopes I am the same. Sincerely, Beth." I grimaced and put the letter away. "Sincerely. Well, she always was a sincere girl."

Lou shook her head. "Don't, Matt."

"I know. Why be bitter? She's being just as nice as she can. Actually, she's a damn nice person, and I'll clobber that damn rancher with one of his own saddles if he doesn't. . . ." I broke off abruptly. After a little, I said, "I guess I'm not the guy to talk about clobbering people. Somebody might think I meant it."

She glanced down at her hands, not speaking. I looked around for the waiter, and he was right there. In that country, waiters really wait. I ordered drinks.

She said, "Martini for you? I warned you about their gin."

I shrugged. "If it kills me, I can't think of a nicer way to die." Then I stopped talking again. Somehow the subject of mayhem and death just seemed to keep cropping up.

Presently she asked, "What happened after I left Kiruna?"

I said, "It was Operation Cover-up, with bells on. Didn't you read the papers? You were a wealthy female American tourist who'd been kidnaped for money by wicked international gangsters. Elin was a brave Swedish girl who was acting as my guide, trying to save you. Who I was wasn't quite clear. The word espionage wasn't mentioned, the subject of photography never came up, and a certain great nation to the east never figured in the deal at all." I glanced at her. "I have a surprise for you. Your article is being published, with pictures."

Her eyes widened. "How did you manage that?"

"After the local authorities had developed the films and cut out everything that might be remotely interesting to a potential enemy, they let me have the scraps that were left. We'd shot quite a bit, you remember, and from time to time I'd picked up a few exposures on my own while you were champing at the bit. Well, going over the stuff, I found enough to work with. The piece will appear in a forthcoming issue, and the editor can't be too displeased with it, since he wrote asking if we'd be interested in working together on another article of a similar nature." I looked at her across the table. "Would we?"

"Why," she said, after the briefest hesitation, "why, it sounds wonderful, Matt. . . ."

We had fish for dinner. They can't cook meat for shucks over here, perhaps because they haven't any worth eating, but they can take anything that swims and turn it into a

174

gourmet's delight. Afterward, I put her in a taxi and took her to her hotel, which didn't happen to be the same as mine, for a change. She didn't hesitate when we reached her door. She just unlocked it and walked in, leaving it open for me to follow, which I did, closing the door behind me. She got rid of her purse and gloves. Her full-skirted dress swished softly as she turned to face me.

"Nice," I said, indicating it with a gesture.

"It's about time you noticed," she said. Then a kind of spark came into her eyes, something spontaneous and mischievous that gave me hope. "It wasn't very expensive," she murmured. "You can rip it if you like."

"The great Kiruna rape scene," I said wryly. "I'm never going to live that down, am I?"

She was silent, smiling, waiting, and there wasn't anything more to say, and I stepped forward, and I didn't really know what the hell to do. I could have been a kid on his first heavy date. I began unfastening her dress buttons, starting at the top. Then, suddenly, she was in my arms, the way it was supposed to be, and everything was going to be all right, everything was going to be fine, and then everything stopped, and that was all there was to that.

She made a small sound in her throat. I let her go and stepped back.

"I'm sorry, Matt," she whispered. "I'm terribly sorry. That's why I . . . I thought if I went away for a while . . . thought I could forget. . . ."

"Sure, kid," I said.

"The man in the bushes with a broken neck," she whispered. "The one by the cabin with a bullet in the back. In the back, Matt!"

"Yeah," I said. "In the back. He happened to be facing that way."

She shook her head desperately. "And Caselius himself. . . . I hated him more than I'd ever hated another human being. But he'd surrendered, Matt! He had his hands in the air!"

I said, "As a boy, I knew a fellow who'd throw rocks at you and call you all kinds of dirty names, and the minute you landed a solid punch, he'd start yelling uncle. He escaped more lickings that way." She shook her head again, in that blind and unreasoning way. I said, "It was my job, Lou. I had to finish it, no matter where his damn hands were. I couldn't leave it for some other poor sap to have to do all over again."

"I know," she whispered. "I know, and I know he was going to kill me and you saved me, but—"

"Yeah," I said. I reached out and fastened the two buttons of her dress I'd undone. "There," I said. "Well, take it easy, doll. There's a guy named Wellington in town, whom you may remember. He's got a cast on and it itches and he'd like sympathy, I'm sure. Look him up. You two ought to have a lot in common. He thinks I'm a stinker, too."

"Matt!" she said. "Matt, I—"

I got out of there, and when I got to my own hotel room, some blocks away, the phone was ringing. I hesitated, but she'd know it was over; she'd have more sense than to call. I went over and picked up the instrument.

"Herr Helm," the desk clerk's voice said, "Herr Helm, you have a transatlantic telephone call, from a Mr. Martin Carrol, in Washington. I will try to get the connection for you. I will call you back."

I hung up. For a blank moment, all I could think of was that I didn't know anybody named Martin Carrol, in Washington or anywhere else. Then I thought of the initials, M.C. for Mac. Cute. I shivered, and wondered what the job would be this time. That was a silly thing to wonder about. I knew what it would be. The only questions were who and where.

The phone rang again. I picked it up. "We are getting your party in Washington, Herr Helm. Are you ready to take the call?"

I didn't answer at once. The funny part was, I couldn't feel a thing about Lou. What I was feeling was about another girl, a girl who'd been beautiful and young and kind of crazy. That was what I really needed, I thought, a girl who was a little crazy. But she was dead.

The clerk's voice held a note of impatience. "Herr Helm, are you ready?"

"Yes," I said. "Yes, I'm ready. . . ."